P9-EJO-022

OPERATION OLEANDER

Valerie O. Patterson

CLARION BOOKS
Houghton Mifflin Harcourt
Boston   New York   2013

With special thanks to my editor, Daniel Nayeri, for patiently watching this book emerge and guiding me along and to my agent, Sarah Davies of Greenhouse Literary for believing in me. To members of my writing group (Ellen, Corey, Erin, Lezlie, Lorrie-Ann, and Sydney), your feedback and friendship have been invaluable. Thanks also to senior editor Jennifer Greene and associate designer Opal Roengchai — and everyone at Clarion — for making this book so beautiful. And to Tom, there aren't enough words to convey my appreciation for your love and friendship.

Clarion Books
215 Park Avenue South
New York, New York 10003

Copyright © 2013 by Valerie O. Patterson

All rights reserved. For information about permission to reproduce selections from this book, write to Permissions, Houghton Mifflin Harcourt Publishing Company, 215 Park Avenue South, New York, New York 10003.

Clarion Books is an imprint of Houghton Mifflin Harcourt Publishing Company.

www.hmhbooks.com

The text was set in Warnock Pro.

Library of Congress Cataloging-in-Publication Data
Patterson, Valerie O.
Operation Oleander / Valerie O. Patterson.
p. cm.
 Summary: Seventh-grader Jess and her friends establish the Order of the Oleander to collect supplies for an orphanage in Kabul, Afghanistan, where two of their parents are deployed, but when disaster strikes and many blame the Order, Jess must find a way to go on.
ISBN 978-0-547-24437-2 (hardback) [1. Charity—Fiction. 2. Orphanages—Fiction. 3. Soldiers—Fiction. 4. Afghan War, 2001—Fiction. 5. Bombings—Fiction. 6. Clubs—Fiction. 7. Afghanistan—History—2001—Fiction.] I. Title.
PZ7.P278152Oth 2013
[Fic]—dc23
 2012023166

Manufactured in the United States of America
DOC 10 9 8 7 6 5 4 3 2 1
4500396370

For my parents,
and for all those who serve

☆

 **ONE**

WHITENESS EXPLODES behind my eyelids, and my eyes shoot open. I'm not sure if I am awake or still asleep and dreaming. My heart beats hard and fast and tight, as if trapped inside a small glass jar.

Light glows around my bedroom shades like a solar eclipse.

It's morning. Early. I'm awake after all.

The noise builds again in the distance. First a crackle. Then a sizzle.

Silence.

Then *boom*.

Boom.

BOOM.

Firecrackers. Just firecrackers.

Somebody down the block with leftovers from last

night's Fourth of July. I lie there in bed, trying to force my heart back to normal.

Across the room, Cara sleeps in her toddler bed. She always wakes up when I try to sneak out of the room in the morning, but now she could sleep through a war zone.

My ears strain to hear anything more. Maybe it's finished. Maybe some dad or military police officer on the block has tracked the kid down and yelled at him.

I don't care.

Just that the noise stopped.

Because, after last night, I hate fireworks. The way the lights flamed in the sky and made people sitting on the beach look like silhouettes of soldiers waiting to go into battle.

The clock radio by the bed blinks 12:00 in red over and over like warning lights on a runway. The power must have gone out overnight. It happens during Florida thunderstorms.

With the clock out, I don't know what time it is. I told Meriwether and Sam I'd meet them at the post exchange, the PX, at eight to staff the booth.

I don't know what time it is in Afghanistan, either.

Rumors of troop movements have spread through the post like a game of telephone. *Have you heard? Surge. Maybe this week.* No one knows what's true.

Already dressed in shorts and a T-shirt, I fling off the thin sheet and dash for the kitchen. I plug in the computer and press the on button, holding it hard until the machine strums to life. The monitor glows for seconds with a gray, empty light. Then the login page appears, and I enter my password.

The screen flickers.

I tap my fingers against the keyboard. *Hurry up.*

In the upper right-hand corner, the time shows. 6:44 a.m.

Late afternoon in Afghanistan.

I click through to my e-mail.

Pressing the icon to get mail is like entering a code that sends Dad's message across a wire from Afghanistan to here, and I imagine cables running undersea, across deserts. As if Dad's physically connected to me by a cord, knotted and strong. Something that can't unravel.

I know it's really just a signal through a satellite. It seems impossible, almost magical. Something not to trust.

Only, his e-mail is there.

I check the date and time of his note. As of this morning, Dad was still alive in Afghanistan. I try not to think about it this way, but I can't help it.

I reach toward the wall and pick up the chewed-end

pencil — Cara's — tied to a string. I mark an X on the calendar for yesterday, July 4. One day less to go before he comes home.

A ritual, marking off the days on a calendar until a whole month, and then another, and another, is crossed out. Only then — it has to be in the proper order — do I open the e-mail message. It's short.

> Dear Jess: I attached a video and some new photos Cpl. Scott and I took at the orphanage. Guess which photos I took. (Hint: They'll be the catawampus ones.) See how great Warda looks? What a difference you all are making. The school supplies are a big hit. Keep them coming.
> Love, Dad
> PS — We roasted hot dogs on the Fourth over the burn pits. The buns were AWOL, but the dogs tasted like home. What I would have done for sparklers.

Sparklers.

Last year, when it got dark enough, Dad brought out sparklers. The bright flowers danced, and the smell of match tips lingered in the air. We ran up and down the beach, waving our wands of light until they fizzled.

Then the real fireworks started. The firemen lit them off a barge towed out into the gulf. The rockets shot into the air. I couldn't see them when they lifted off, but you could hear them. The swoosh of power jetting them up, followed by silence until they burst overhead. Green and red and blue and white sparkles showering the sky. Dad said the blue was the rarest color. I forget why.

I open the attached photo, and my hand squeezes the computer mouse. Warda's photo. Her wide green eyes are like those of the Afghani girl from an old *National Geographic* magazine Ms. Rivera tacked to the bulletin board at school. She said it was taken when Soviet troops invaded Afghanistan. Gunships fired on villages, and bombs disguised as toys glittered in the village roads, tempting children to pluck them off the ground like piñata candy.

Warda's eyes are just like those from the other photo. Startled, haunting, seeing more than they can express. As if there's something just beyond the reach of the camera, something she can't forget. They're like the photo I found in an old album in the utility closet after we moved on post. A photo with curled edges. A girl wearing a faded T-shirt and a hat, haunted eyes staring out. Mine.

In this shot, Warda stands straight, stiff, facing forward. Dad's on one side of her, and Meriwether's mother, Corporal Scott, kneels on the other side of Warda and smiles. But it is Warda's eyes that draw me in, and somehow her eyes are my eyes. I am the girl thousands of miles away in an orphanage, Dad's hand on my shoulder. And I am safe.

I download the other photos and the video of the children playing in the courtyard, the milk goat we raised money for grazing on weeds in the background. We named it Zebah. It's a name that's easy to say. Sam and I dig deep inside for a voice that rumbles out into a big long *zzzz* sound when we pronounce it.

Against the pockmarked building, oleander bushes battle to survive. Dad said they bloom in the same shades as here. That's what gave me the idea for Operation Oleander, the plan to donate supplies to the orphanage. It's why I'm meeting Meriwether and Sam at the PX so early. I print out the photos and upload the video to my MP3 player so people get to see what they're supporting.

I type a reply.

Dear Dad:
Great photos. Our hot dogs had buns.

I don't say we didn't go to the post fireworks, that we stayed home. I don't ask about the surge and if it's started. Instead I write,

Remember the fireworks last year? How perfect they were? Love, Jess.

I hit the send button and let my fingers linger over the keys. Feel the connection being made and the message reaching back across the distance to Dad.

Inside the house, everything is quiet. No more fire-crackers. No more booms. No noise comes from my bed-room. Cara is still asleep, and Mom's door is shut tight.

I sign off the computer, make sure Mom's coffeepot is programmed to brew at eight, grab my iPod, and head out the door. When the key clicks in the lock, I rattle the doorknob just to make sure it's secure before I walk toward the PX.

TWO

FOG CLINGS to the tops of the pines and palm trees lining the streets of the Fort Spencer Army Post housing area. Spider webs gleam wet along the chainlink fences and in the thick bougainvillea at the house on the corner. Pine straw and torn leaves from last night's storm mingle with bits of soggy red paper. Leftovers from someone's ticker tape. But no one's around. Whoever set off the explosions has retreated like an unseen enemy.

A few cars are parked outside the PX when I get there. The doors, cloudy with condensation, whoosh open, and I step into the corridor. It doesn't look like much. Just like a mall before the stores open. Kids' artwork plasters almond-color walls, and slick tile floors echo when I walk through, even in flip-flops. But the hallway is the perfect location. Anyone who shops on post walks through these doors.

We're ready for them.

I'm unpacking the storage closet in the manager's office off the hallway next to the PX when Meriwether strolls in. She yawns and pulls the sleeves of her pink hoodie below her fingers as if it's winter. That's summer in Florida—hot and humid outside and pneumonia-cold inside.

"You're early." I unload a box of chips and pretzels onto the table.

"Don't get used to it," Meriwether says. "Dad was called in. Some computer glitch. He dropped me off. Promised to bring frappés back." She grins from under her hood. Meriwether's dad works on post as a civilian.

"For me, too?"

"That's what he said. You know he likes you more than me." Meriwether folds her arms and shivers. She stamps her feet as if it were February and snowing. Not that it does that in Clementine, Florida. Ever.

"He does not." But inside I smile. Mr. Scott's very nice. He just doesn't know what to do with Meriwether sometimes. He acts like she's some sort of complex rope puzzle he can't solve now that Mrs. Scott has been deployed.

"Is Sam coming?" she asks.

"He's supposed to." Sometimes Sam makes excuses not to come to the PX to help out. He acts embarrassed to be asking for contributions to charity. Or maybe he's uncomfortable hanging out with enlisted soldiers' kids like Meriwether and me.

"He'd better come." Meriwether unfolds three metal chairs, one for each of us, and plants them behind the table where we sit down.

"You just want him to introduce you to Caden." Caden is a junior lifeguard at the post pool. He was in our class last year, but he didn't talk to Meriwether or me unless he had to for a school assignment.

"Not true." But the corners of her lips curl up.

I can tell she's about to start talking about him, so I say, "Come look. Dad sent some new photos. Your mom took some of them. There's new video, too." I pull up the album. "There's Warda and your mom." I point to the photo of Warda with my dad and Meriwether's mother.

"Where?" Meriwether pushes back her hood and swishes her blond hair over her shoulder. She leans over the iPod and squints.

"Why don't you just wear your glasses?"

"I'm working on Dad to get me contacts."

That means she'll get them. Eventually.

"Well, what do you think?" I hold my breath. I think

it's the best photo yet. That we'll take in lots of donations as a result. I want her to be as excited as I am. "See how much better they all look?"

Meriwether doesn't answer right away.

My breath leaks out, like a punctured bike tire.

She bends closer, until her face almost touches the screen.

"Don't you see how much healthier Warda looks, how she's finally smiling?" I ask.

"You think so? She still doesn't have any shoes on."

"What?" I search the photo. I hadn't noticed Warda's bare feet. I'd just seen her eyes. They drew me like perfect moon shells on the beach.

"But the school and the food. You have to see the goat," I say.

Meriwether scoots her chair away from the table. "Oh, no, you don't, Jess Westmark. I see what you're trying to do. We agreed to do this for two months. You forced me into it, remember? You said we'd have the rest of the summer to ourselves. For the pool. The beach. First it was a goat. Then school supplies. No more. You promised." Meriwether folds her arms.

"But, Meriwether, just think . . ."

"No, I mean it. Oceanography camp's in August, and school starts at the end of August. That's *next month*. We collected enough school supplies for a year. And Sam promised to take us sailing. Maybe with you-know-who. I don't want to be stuck in this hallway till oceanography camp."

"I know it's boring," I say. But it's not, really. Not when you have a mission.

"No kidding." Meriwether sits there all hunched over, frowning, and I'm just feet from her, close enough to touch her arm. It scares me, how we can be so close and so far away from each other at the same time.

Finally, Meriwether grabs my arms and pulls me to my feet. "Okay, Jess, let's just do this. The sooner we set up today, the sooner we're out of here."

"Okay, okay." I surrender. But I'm smiling.

Meriwether centers the tablecloth and lines up packages of chips and cookies in decorative baskets we took from her house weeks ago. "Mom won't miss these. Not for another six months," she said. *Until the end of deployment.* That's what Meriwether didn't say out loud.

There are lots of things we don't say aloud anymore.

I prop up the poster about Operation Oleander and our efforts to support the orphanage in Afghanistan. Updated photos go into the album display.

"You know, your mom took some of these." I point to some of the pictures in the album.

Meriwether focuses. "She did?" She studies them as if she can figure something out about her mom by looking at the photos she took.

"Good morning, ladies." Ms. Rivera, our English teacher from eighth grade last year, stands at our table. "Hope your summer reading is going well."

"Hi," Meriwether and I say together, and nod.

"How's it coming?" Ms. Rivera points toward our display.

"Okay," I say. "We're making one more push, you know, this month." I want to say we'll keep supporting the orphanage into the fall. Next to me, though, Meriwether fidgets with the poster, straightening it.

"Yes. The rest of July," Meriwether says. *And no longer,* she means.

Ms. Rivera nods at the photo of Warda and Dad and Corporal Scott.

"Jess, you look so much like your dad."

My smile freezes to my face. *Not really.* We both have gray eyes. But my face is shaped like a heart, and his is large and oval. He freckles and I tan. Meriwether bumps my knee under the table, breaking the winter ice sealing my lips together.

"Cara really looks like him." She has the same cowlick where her part goes, the same oval face, skin so pale it looks see-through in the sun.

"She must be adorable now," Ms. Rivera says, and drops five dollars and a packet of watercolor pencils into the donation basket.

"She is." When she's not being a brat. "Thank you." I push away what Ms. Rivera said and reach under the table for a box. "Oh, I forgot to put the flowers out. Do you want one? Any contributor gets one." I pull out the paper oleanders I'd made.

"Sure," Ms. Rivera says as a couple walks toward the table.

I hand one to her, then arrange the rest in a clear plastic vase. We need another pack of pink and white tissue paper to make more. Just folding the paper makes me feel good. The softness under my fingers. When the tissue flowers open, they seem to bloom in my hands.

"I'd better run. Looks like you have some more potential donors." Ms. Rivera winks and hurries away.

As the couple approaches, I can see the man's dressed in tan-brown fatigues. The woman wears a sundress, and she rests her hand over her belly, protecting it.

She reminds me of when Mom was pregnant with Cara over three years ago. How the fear crawled under my skin and I didn't want to look at her. The baby would be part of a circle I couldn't ever enter. Mom and Dad hadn't stopped loving me when Cara was born, but things sneak up on you like speeding cars and train wrecks. Worry creeps in like trumpet vine.

"Hello," the woman says.

"Would you like to help?" I start into my memorized speech. "We're supporting the girls' orphanage in Kabul. Since January we've sponsored a milk goat and sent school supplies. We've had concrete results." *Concrete results* — that's what adults call success.

The man shifts on his heels, but the woman edges closer. She's drawn to the photos, I can tell.

"Look, honey. See this girl?" the woman says.

"Yes," I say. I start to tell her the story about Warda, but the man is frowning.

"We'd better hurry," he says.

His arm brushes the poster as he touches his wife's shoulder and steers her away. The poster slides off the tripod and floats toward the floor. The man doesn't notice. He's only looking at his wife. He acts like something can go wrong with her baby just by her looking at photos of orphans.

Meriwether reaches for the poster, but she misses. For a second I am falling with it, but Meriwether reaches down and retrieves it from the floor.

"He didn't want to be here," she says under her breath to me, and straightens the poster back on its stand.

"No," I say, breathing again. But it was more than that. He didn't want *us* to be here.

I rearrange the paper oleanders, positioning them as if they're real flowers going into fresh water. Then I place the vase next to the poster so people can't miss the oleanders.

So they can't dismiss our mission.

THREE

OTHER PEOPLE begin to arrive. Mothers walk by with toddlers in tow. Kids with money in their pockets park their bikes and dash inside to spend it. Meriwether and I smile at everyone. Some people pause long enough to check out the photos at our table. A few coming out of the PX drop pads of paper or colored pencils into the basket.

Every time a donation lands on the table, I smile like the Salvation Army bell ringers at Christmas. Even when someone looks at the photos and walks away without donating, I make myself say, "Thank you for coming by." My cheeks hurt from smiling. Not everyone can give. Not everyone wants to give.

When people just walk away, though, it bothers me.

Still, no one acts like the man who knocked over the poster.

Meriwether reaches into a box under the table and refills empty spots in the baskets. "If Sam doesn't come . . ."

"He said he was coming." I believe him. Really. To him, "duty, honor, country" aren't just three words. At least, if it doesn't mean contradicting his dad.

"But he's not here."

I shrug. "Call him."

"I'll wait." Meriwether sighs and sits at the table with her chin in her hands. She fluffs the packages of chips. "Maybe Caden will come by."

A couple of army officers walk up.

"Good morning, ladies. I'll take a soda. Here, keep the change," one of them says, handing me a five-dollar bill. That means another box of pencils and then some. Maybe we'll have enough to send a large tin of colored pencils. Not just the eight-pack of basic colors but the set of ninety-eight, with names like sepia and scarlet tanager.

"Thanks," Meriwether says, and reaches into the cooler for a can.

"I'll take some chips, too," he says.

"Nice breakfast," his companion says.

The first man shrugs. "I had cold pizza yesterday. It's been one of those weeks."

"We'd better get going." The other man's voice is tight and narrow, as if he doesn't trust himself to say much. He sounds like he's already in the office checking computers and orders and maps of the war, or whatever he does there. But he fishes for change anyway and drops some coins into our basket. "Thanks, ladies. Keep up the good work."

"We will," Meriwether says, sitting straight and tall in her chair. As if our mission had been her idea.

I tease her after they leave. "We?"

Meriwether ignores me and tosses her hair. She grins. "Okay, I know. But I'm helping. More than Sam."

"That wouldn't be hard." I move the baskets so they're straight, with their corners touching. Orderly, like the army. The way Dad would arrange things.

Meriwether grabs my arm. "There he is."

Only Meriwether could conjure up a boy just by wishing him there. She sits in her chair acting like she doesn't see him.

"What's he doing?" she asks.

"What do you think he's doing? This is the way to the PX."

I wave at Caden, trying to get his attention.

Meriwether yanks on the hem of my shorts. "What are you doing?"

"Trying to get him to come over."

"Don't do that!" Meriwether tugs on my shorts until I sit down, hard, in the folding chair.

Caden walks by, not looking our way.

"Meriwether, you're never going to talk to him if — "

Outside, a car screeches to a halt. I cringe as the sound echoes through the long hallway. The sliding glass doors part, and a figure runs through.

It's Meriwether's dad.

Meriwether drops the iPod on the table. "He didn't bring the frappés."

Mr. Scott dashes toward our table. I stand up, but that's all I can do. Everything around us seems more intense. The chill in the hall. The glare from outside as the sliding doors open to admit shoppers. When Mr. Scott reaches us, he looks lost. For a second the wide, startled expression in his eyes reminds me of Warda.

"Dad?" Meriwether asks.

"Come on. We've got to go home."

Meriwether doesn't move. She sits there as if caught in an undertow and unable to swim to shore.

"What's wrong?" I ask.

"A bombing," he says. "I heard on the radio. Back in the office. Meriwether, come on. We need to get home now. See what the networks are saying."

"I can't. I just got here to help Jess." Meriwether folds her arms.

"Bombing? Where?" I ask.

"Kabul," Mr. Scott says as if I'm an idiot. That of course a bombing occurred there. As if a bomb could have exploded anywhere else. "Come on, Meriwether."

Last month a market in Kabul was bombed. The television talked about women and children dying. That's probably what's happened this time — another market attack.

"Go." I nudge Meriwether out of her chair. "Just go. I'll put this stuff away."

"Are you sure?"

"Yes, it's okay."

"You should go home too, Jess. We can drop you," Mr. Scott says. My street comes before theirs in the housing area. But he's already backing toward the door, even as he looks to me to answer.

"That's okay. I'll follow you." I can't leave things where they are. Dad always says, "Duty first."

Straighten up.

Stay calm.

Keep order.

Put everything away.

Mr. Scott nods and speeds toward the exit.

Meriwether mumbles under her breath, and I hear her say Caden's name. But she sprints after her dad.

Seconds later, the car squeals away.

Mothers with their children are pushing full grocery carts from the PX. They look sideways at me as they rumble like tanks toward the parking lot. With their eyes they ask if there's anything they should worry about.

Don't panic. I make myself slow down. Pick up the storage boxes one at a time. At least, I do while they're looking, because I don't want to upset them. Because that's what military families do: they stay calm, even in an emergency. Dad would say that, too.

As soon as they exit, though, I stuff bags of chips and snacks into boxes. I don't care if they're mixed up.

A bomb.

Maybe Mr. Scott heard it all wrong.

"Jess!"

Sam's marching toward me. Even when he doesn't run, his walk covers a lot of ground. I have to jog to keep up with him on a regular day.

Today he walks even faster. But he, too, projects calm and order, even though tension pulses just under his skin. I can tell by the way he holds his arms at his sides. Like a soldier.

"Now you show up." I slam the rest of the snacks into boxes.

"Don't be mad. I was going to come earlier. Honest. But something's happened." Sam's face is damp from sweat, from the heat.

"I don't want to hear it."

He touches my arm. "Come on. It's important."

I snatch it away and step back from the table.

"There's been a bombing," he says. "The TV says Fort Spencer troops are involved. Mom drove me here so I could tell you."

The cool air makes my chest ache. Mr. Scott didn't say anything about Fort Spencer troops.

I wait for him to continue. Through the glass doors behind him, Sam's mother must be sitting in her air-conditioned car.

"It was in Kabul, Jess. I have to go. Mom's waiting. We can give you a ride."

"No, I can't go yet. Meriwether's dad came and got her." All the things left on the table still. The poster of Dad and Meriwether's mom and Warda.

"Let me help you," he says, grabbing snacks and slapping them into a half-filled box.

"No." I seize the box.

He stands there looking lost the way Mr. Scott did.

"I can do it," I say.

He doesn't argue with me.

"I'll call you later," he says.

I want him to argue with me, but he's already through the doors and gone into the July heat that shimmers over the asphalt like waves of dark water.

How many hours since Dad wrote? Did he write as soon as he heard about the bombing? So we wouldn't worry?

Kabul.

Troops.

Bomb.

The words swirl in my head.

I cram the snack boxes onto a shelf in the storage closet. Pretzel bags mix with chips. Candy bars jostle out of their trays. I tug, but I can't lift the cooler with the ice in it.

I can't leave it. It belongs to Sam's family. I drag it to the side door, turn it upside down. Ice and cans spill onto the fresh-cut grass outside. One at a time, I grab the sodas and toss them back into the cooler. Each one thuds against the hard plastic sides like my heart against my chest. Bits of cut grass stick to the slippery cans and the bottom of my flip-flops, but I don't stop to brush them off.

I push the cooler inside the closet and slam the door, the key in both my hands, which are still wet from the grass and ice. I fumble with the lock. Finally, it catches, and I yank out the key. I grab my iPod.

When I run through the doors, the white light sears my skin.

Home.

FOUR

THE HOUSING area seems so ordinary. No sirens blaring. No police cars speeding by with blazing lights. Instead, automatic sprinklers whir across magazine-perfect lawns. Hibiscus bushes bloom, and oleander. I skip the cracks in the sidewalk just like Cara does.

A flock of monk parakeets spirals overhead, heading toward the grove of guava trees behind the parade ground. At the height of guava season, the birds sound like monkeys screeching. Teenagers scare little kids into thinking the trees are haunted.

Just the tattered red paper reminds me yesterday was the Fourth of July.

Maybe the early damage reports were wrong. Maybe Mr. Scott and Sam worried for nothing. Maybe I'll get home and find out it's all a mistake. False alarms happen a lot in a war zone. Right?

If Fort Spencer troops are affected, why isn't everybody in full gear? Isn't that what army posts do in a crisis? Mobilize? Even if the crisis is halfway across the world?

Check e-mail for any more news from Dad. He'd write as soon as he could. Already maybe there's a message there, waiting for me.

Don't trip over your flip-flops. Concentrate on street names. Don't panic. North–south streets are presidents, like Lincoln and Monroe. Lisbon and Canton, cities, run east–west. On the coast, the Gulf of Mexico cuts into the post like a scimitar, leaving a curved scar on the beach. Sometimes the South Seas Road washes out along the shoreline near the airstrip and parade ground.

I cut the corner on Madrid Street and look for my house half a block down. When we moved in, the administrative office called the concrete blockhouses "historic bungalows." Mom called them "matchboxes." Small and look-alike. Maybe one house has a carport on the right side and another has one on the left. Or maybe the trim's painted a different color — army green or battleship gray. At first I could only find my house by the number 306 spray-painted on the curb. Or by seeing Cara's big tricycle on its side in the driveway.

That was last year. Now I can find it even if I'm running in the dusk of summer, flying ahead of mosquitoes, the sound of Meriwether laughing about a boy at the pool still in my ears.

Straining to see my house, I pretend I'm looking at it for the first time. That it belongs to another military family and the gray house trimmed in green is unfamiliar. And I've never seen the green mold almost the same shade as the trim growing on the outside, near the drainpipes. That I don't know about how the jalousie windows in the living room don't close all the way or that at night, or after a rain, palmetto bugs slip in through the cracks. With Dad deployed, it's my job to be brave and kill them so Mom doesn't have to. So Cara doesn't scream when she finds them crawling in the kitchen.

Across the street, Mrs. Johnson's sprinkler's turned off. Despite the brightness, her curtains hang wide open. That usually means she's peering out to see what's happening. She always knows when our neighbor's dog does his business near her mailbox.

I unlock the door, half expecting to see Mrs. Johnson sitting on the sofa, drinking coffee out of Dad's Texas Rangers mug. She's over almost every day.

No Mrs. Johnson. Not yet anyway.

I plug in the computer in the kitchen and hit the on button. In the living room, I grab the remote and punch on the television, holding the volume down. Everything in the house sits quietly, waiting. Mom and Cara must still be asleep.

I won't wake Mom yet. Not till I know there's something to worry about for real.

Troops.

Bomb.

The words in my head repeat like music that won't stop.

Images on the television appear smoky and unclear. They don't have all the details. It's a developing news story. At the bottom of the screen the words "breaking news" blare in red letters. Smoke rises from a street area in the hazy background.

I press the volume button.

"A massive car bombing has damaged a Kabul neighborhood near a market destroyed weeks ago, in what appears to be a larger, better-coordinated attack on infrastructure. Fire still rages in the streets. Civilians, including children, and possibly U.S. soldiers reportedly are among the dead. A U.S. Army Humvee has been destroyed in the attack."

The station breaks for a commercial. I dash into the kitchen to check e-mail. No new e-mail. I press refresh and look again. Nothing. Maybe Dad hasn't heard anything. Or, more likely, they're on lockdown after the explosion. Maybe he couldn't get to a computer to send an all-clear message.

I dial Sam's number.

Busy.

Then I try Meriwether's number. It, too, rings busy. It's like when the hurricane hit last fall and everyone got on their phones after the worst was over to tell relatives they were okay. The phone service got overloaded. Just busy signals for hours.

In the living room, I jab the controls, searching for another channel. There has to be more information. One exclusive shows the actual explosion, which was captured by chance by a man who had been reporting on educational statistics. The replay reveals a static city scene glimmering in the distance. In the foreground, palm fronds wave in the sunny late afternoon. Wind ruffles the reporter's hair.

Without warning, the screen rips apart. For a second the flash of an explosion consumes everything, and I can't turn away or close my eyes. The reporter crouches, covering his ears, and for a second drops the microphone. The footage shimmers as if an earthquake is upending everything.

I squeeze my eyes shut. The red and white streamers from the fireworks reflect against the back of my eyelids.

The sound of the explosion rockets through my eardrums. The scene on television reminds me of last night on the beach, the way the silhouettes made everyone look like soldiers. I was afraid, afraid for Dad and everyone in the unit. It was just a moment, a flash, and then I tried to brush it away like sand off my legs.

On television, smoke and dust are all I can see.

The anchor cuts away. "We'll be back with more on this unfolding story."

The scene changes to a cat food commercial.

The phone rings, and I snatch it off the receiver.

"Meriwether?"

"It's Sam."

"I tried to call you," I say. "My mom's still asleep. What's happening?" He has to know something, or he wouldn't call. He won't let what he thinks about Operation Oleander stop him from doing the right thing. From telling me what he can.

"The major offensive. It's started. Troops are moving south." Sam's voice sounds like a television reporter's. Neutral and practiced. "A car bombing got part of the unit before they could join the convoy. They'd stopped at an orphanage."

Orphanage.

The word reverberates in my head.

"Ours?"

For a moment he doesn't answer.

"Yes." His voice drops as if he's telling me something he shouldn't.

"Casualties?"

"Yes." We talk as if in Morse code: clipped, in as few words as possible.

"Soldiers, too?"

"Yes."

"Who?"

Again Sam is silent. The emptiness inside the receiver deafens me.

I close my eyes. He knows. He has to know. His dad is Commander Butler. He'd get word here first. Even though he's here now, not in Afghanistan, he'll know, since the soldiers are from Fort Spencer.

Opening my eyes, I check the muted television screen again. Smoke curls toward the late-afternoon sky. People behind the announcer run back and forth on streets crowded with honking cars jammed at all angles like Cara's toy trucks. A man dodges through the chaos, a child limp in his arms.

"Sam. Tell me. Who?" Was that why he came to the PX? Because he knew then but he couldn't tell me? And he still can't tell me?

"I don't know." He evades me like Cara does when she's taken one of my gel pens without asking.

"You do know. Who's injured? Tell me." I can't ask if anyone's dead. I can't get those words out. I won't think them.

"I'd better go."

"Is it my dad?" I rush to get the words in before he hangs up.

"I'm not sure. I wasn't supposed to hear anything. I was standing outside the living room when the colonel came to talk to my dad. Dad barely had time to get dressed, and then he ran out."

"You don't know about my dad? Really?"

"I don't."

"What about our orphanage?"

"What do you mean, 'ours'?"

"Yes, ours," I say. We sent pencils and paper. Contributed toward food. "Even you."

"I helped. I got us the space, didn't I?" he asks, his voice rising.

He did.

"Yes, but you haven't been around much," I tell him. Not ever since Mrs. Johnson complained that the operation is unsupportive of our troops and we shouldn't spend that kind of effort on the orphanage.

"I said I was sorry about that."

Behind me, I hear stirring from Mom's bedroom.

"I have to go. Mom's up. Sam, what about Warda?"

"I don't know. Really." His voice pleads for me to be-lieve him.

I hang up and turn off the television, the screen nar-rowing to blackness, then prop myself up on the couch, my back to the wall. Mom's coming down the hallway. Her slippers sound like palm fronds rustling in the breeze.

What will I say?

Mom stops at the doorway to the living room. Her hair's not brushed. She squints as if half-asleep. She says that with Dad gone she stays up too late at night. She turns on her headphones and listens to music until she falls asleep.

"Jess? Who was that?"

No one, I almost say. That way, maybe Mom won't have to know something's happened. Maybe in a few hours the news will be clearer. Dad will call.

"Jess!"

"Sam. It was Sam."

"This early? What time is it, anyway?" Mom fumbles for the light switch.

"It's not that early." I don't bother to tell her I've been to the PX already. She knows that's where I go. She doesn't really like me going so early, before so I try to keep quiet. To fly under the radar.

A knock sounds on the door.

I freeze. I didn't hear a car door slam, like in one of

those old World War II movies Dad used to watch. The car is always black. It creeps down the street, stopping in front of some unlucky family's house. Someone inside pulls back a curtain. The camera pans so that you see the military officer walk slowly up to the front door and knock. They never use the doorbell. They always knock.

"What's going on around here?" Mom's voice sounds sharp, more awake.

I stay still. If I don't move, this might pass.

"I swear, Jess." Mom runs her fingers through her hair and straightens her sleep T-shirt so it covers her thighs. She cracks open the door, and we both squint against the sudden light.

"I came as soon as I heard." Mrs. Johnson pushes inside, carrying a box of glazed doughnuts. The sweet scent makes me dizzy.

"I went down to the gas station," she says. "I got us some snacks and tried to get the latest news from Pops. He knows everything."

So that's where Mrs. Johnson was — getting the gossip. I should have known.

"Heard what?" Mom asks.

Mrs. Johnson stops midstride from where she was going to plant herself in Dad's recliner. "You don't know? Really?"

"Know what?" Mom makes an exasperated sound.

"People sneaking around at all hours of the morning. Yet no one says anything." She frowns at me.

I hug myself.

"Turn on the television, Jess," Mrs. Johnson says. She turns to my mom. "You got coffee brewing?"

Mom starts to say "No."

"It brewed at eight this morning," I said. "I programmed the coffee maker." I wanted Mom to know I could help out — that's why I started setting the coffee to go on automatically in the mornings. Just lately, since summer started, Mom's been sleeping in later and later. Until the coffee smell turns bitter. Sometimes I toast waffles for Cara's breakfast.

"Well, that'll be strong enough to walk to Cuba," Mrs. Johnson says. "I'll brew fresh. You stay here." Mrs. Johnson steers Mom to Dad's recliner and stalks into the kitchen. I hear her turn on the water and pour all the coffee I already made down the drain. The new canister of the ground coffee hisses when she opens the lid. Mrs. Johnson knows our kitchen so well, she doesn't have to ask anymore where to find things.

Mom sinks into the recliner.

"Turn it on, Jess."

I grip the remote. I hold it toward the television.

"Do it!"

I hit the button, and the screen jolts into view. This

time there aren't any immediate reruns of the bomb going off. I'm glad Mom doesn't have to see that first thing.

I click through the channels, looking for another station. One of Clementine's newscasters has broken into local programming to announce the offensive and that casualties have been reported. A camera shot displays the main gate at Fort Spencer, flags flying and guards checking identification as people drive onto the post. Military ID checks are routine, but seeing them on television makes them seem ominous, as if the guards expect an attack on post the way the soldiers overseas do.

"What happened?" Mom asks.

"A bombing," I say.

"Near that orphanage," Mrs. Johnson says as she comes into the living room.

Mrs. Johnson can't wait to tell Mom it's about the orphanage. She never liked the idea of what we're doing. *No good will come of it.* Those had been her words exactly.

The local channel doesn't have any names either. Or they aren't saying. They don't even show the footage of the bomb going off.

"Put on CNN," Mrs. Johnson says.

I speed through the channels. There the view's familiar. The reporter standing on the street, unaware of what's about to happen. It's worse this time because I know what's coming. People walk back and forth in the background. A stray dog digs through garbage.

The calm before the bomb.

My fingers ache to hit the off button.

"Turn it up," Mom says, her voice stronger.

"You don't — "

"Jess!"

I spike the volume. The reporter talking to the camera, the palms waving in the breeze. Let me turn the scene off before it explodes, I plead silently like a prayer. Let me freeze the moment in time so that it never happens.

But it's too late.

FIVE

WE SIT in front of the television like a family in a hospital waiting room. Mom in Dad's recliner. Mrs. Johnson and me on opposite ends of the sofa. We are numb, mute. No one moves. We breathe too softly to hear ourselves. If we inhale too hard, we will take in smoke and fire. That's how close we are to the explosion.

Mom reacts first. She yanks the remote control out of my hand and clicks it off. The screen goes dark. Then Mom drops the remote, as if it's an improvised explosive device, an IED that might go off in her hand. It clatters onto the coffee table.

We sit and stare.

"Frank called me," Mrs. Johnson says after a long time.

I frown at Mrs. Johnson. Her husband's already

called? From the war zone? During a surge? Isn't that a violation of orders?

And if he called, why not Dad?

"We've taken casualties," Mrs. Johnson says.

"Who?" Mom asks.

"It's not clear yet. Not entirely. But Frank says some of the unit had stopped by the orphanage. To deliver supplies."

The red numbers on the clock burn my eyes.

"W-Warren?" Mom asks.

"He went in the Humvee."

The Humvee smoldering in the background, too far away for the camera to get a close-up.

Mom fumbles for the remote and turns on the television again.

We watch the replay. We can't help it. Maybe this time something different will happen. Perhaps this time I'll see a clue about who was there.

"What else did Frank say?" Mom's voice sounds flat as water.

Mrs. Johnson closes her eyes, and then opens them. "Maybe we shouldn't talk about this . . ." Her gaze flickers to me. "Jess, why don't you check on your sister?"

"I'm not leaving. I want to hear."

Mom starts to cross her arms, and then her shoulders sag. "Go ahead."

"They had half an hour," Mrs. Johnson says. "Before they headed out."

From down the hall, Cara's three-year-old happy morning voice is singing "Twinkle, Twinkle, Little Star." In a minute she'll be calling for me to read her favorite book, a worn-edged copy, about a caribou that gets lost and then found in the cold northern winter. No matter how many times I've read it to her, she sits there wide-eyed all the way through, as if the ending might change. As if the caribou might be lost forever. But, on the very last page, she'll touch the caribou's antlers to prove to herself it's safe. Then she'll want cartoons while Mom makes breakfast.

Mom jumps up. She wipes her eyes, even though they're dry.

"Turn that off, Jess."

Closest to the television, I hit the power button.

She goes into the kitchen. Mrs. Johnson pushes herself off the sofa and grabs their coffee cups.

I sit in the living room. Down the street a lawn mower sputters to life. I hear every noise, as if I have super hearing.

"Why don't they tell us something?" Mom's voice carries.

"No news is good news."

"Do you believe that?" Mom asks.

"Yes. But it's too soon to know anything. Really." For once Mrs. Johnson's voice doesn't sound happy fake. She says it out plain.

"Or they just can't tell. Maybe they can't identify him." Mom's voice catches. "And I thought that orphanage project was a good thing. Good for Warren. Good for Jess. To give them something to do together. Helping other orphans." Mom's voice sounds ragged. Holding-back-tears ragged. *Other orphans. Like me.* "He's so far away."

Mrs. Johnson murmurs something. I can't tell what.

Down the hall, a voice. "Jess-ie?" Cara calls me that. Jess-E.

I am caught there. Any minute now Cara will call my name again, and then she'll lumber down the hallway dragging her book. Her clothes will be inside out or unmatched. Her funny cowlick will make her hair stick up in back, just like Dad's.

I shiver in the sudden cold of the air-conditioned room.

Dad and others at the orphanage. Delivering goods from Operation Oleander. Supplies we sent.

I spring into the kitchen. Mom's eyes are red-rimmed. Her hands clutch her coffee cup as if it can warm her.

"Why don't you say it?"

"Jess, now . . ." Mrs. Johnson starts. She's sitting at the kitchen table, her arms propping up her head.

I won't look at her. I only see Mom.

"Say what?" Mom asks.

"You think Dad's dead."

"Jess, stop it," Mom says, shaking her head. "We don't know anything. Remember what your dad said?"

I remember everything he said. How to turn off the main water into the house. How to add gas to the lawn mower. To always wear shoes, not flip-flops, if I mow the lawn. To be a good soldier. *Be steadfast.*

The coffeepot gurgles, and a last puff of bitter aroma leaks into the room.

"Jess-E." The voice is coming down the hall.

Everything swirls together. The scent of Mom's coffee. Cara's singsong voice. I can't breathe.

Suddenly, a fierce cramp hits my middle. *Take care of Cara.* Dad's last words to me before he boarded the silver transport plane and I watched the plane fly away until it was just a tiny sparkle like one of the jewels in Cara's caribou book.

The air in the kitchen is too thick.

Cara is marching down the hallway. Closer. I have to get out. Maybe Sam will know something.

I bolt out the kitchen door, onto the driveway.

"Jess!" Mom's voice tails me, but I shake it.

★ ★ ★

The commander lives in the largest house on post. Most of the other houses sit in rows and have tiny, square backyards inside chainlink fences. Here, a long sweeping driveway leads up to the two-story white house on an unfenced green lawn that stands out alone near the water like a lighthouse. Boats on the bay use the house as a landmark, Sam says. On my walks down to the point and back, I look at the house from the shore. Up close, I see that the front porch is bigger than our living room. Tall white columns support the roof.

I catch my breath and ring the doorbell under the shade of the porch. Sam's mother opens the door before the ding-dong sound fades to nothing.

"Jess," she says. "Oh, dear, come in."

By her face, I know she's heard something.

"Sam's upstairs," she says. "Have a seat. Do you want some tea?"

"No, thanks." I slide into a wing chair in the living room. The golden fabric envelops me as I sink into it.

Mrs. Butler walks upstairs. Then she comes back down and disappears into the kitchen.

I want to close my eyes. Just for a minute. But when I do, bursts of light flash against my eyelids.

Sam thunders down the stairs.

"Jess," he says.

"What do you know?"

Sam stands in the living room doorway, as if bracing for an earthquake. Maybe he thinks the solid door frame will keep him safe.

He shifts his weight.

"Sam—"

"Dad's waiting for word now. He said he'll call when he can."

I stare at Sam's face, trying to tell if he's lying. He's not looking me in the eye. He focuses past me on a lamp-shade, on the edge of the wing chair. Anywhere but my face.

Isn't that a sign?

Mrs. Butler carries a tray in from the kitchen. Fluted glasses of orange juice sit on it, and a basket of scones. "Have you had breakfast, Jess?"

Breakfast? I don't remember. I shake my head.

"Please eat something. Even if you think you're not hungry." Mrs. Butler speaks softly, but she won't give up. I know that about her. Sam's dad might be the commander of troops on Fort Spencer, but his mom's in charge of everything else, including Commander Butler.

"Thank you, ma'am." I lift a glass of juice off the tray. Mrs. Butler sets the tray down on the glass coffee table and wraps a scone in a napkin and hands it to me. The warmth of it seeps through the napkin, and I smell the blueberries and melted sugar.

"Nothing better than a hot scone." She passes one to Sam, too, before returning to the kitchen, and he gulps it down. I think how nice Mrs. Butler is and how she always makes Meriwether and me feel welcome. Even though our parents aren't officers.

Meriwether. I need to call her again.

I nibble the edge of the scone. I chew. It doesn't taste like anything, despite how good it smells. I swallow, though, like Mrs. Butler told me to.

"What if he's dead?" I ask Sam.

He frowns. "Don't say that. We don't know yet." He sounds calm and practical like Commander Butler. Not twisted and raw inside the way I am.

"But they targeted them, right? When they went to the orphanage?"

Sam wads his napkin into a ball. "Maybe the Taliban were after the girls' orphanage. Maybe it was bad luck, the soldiers being there then."

Why would they target an orphanage?

Because . . .

The juice sours on my tongue.

Because the soldiers were delivering supplies.

A phone rings in another room. Mrs. Butler answers

it in her calm way. I watch her through the open door into the kitchen.

"Yes, she's here." Mrs. Butler doesn't whisper. She speaks matter-of-factly.

We look at each other, Sam and me. It's Mom. She'd have known I'd come here to Sam's. If I wasn't at Meriwether's.

"No, she's fine. I'm trying to get her to eat a little breakfast." She pauses. "That's okay. No problem at all. I'll drive her home in a few minutes. Please, don't you worry. It's not a bother." Mrs. Butler has her back to us. Phone to her ear, she's staring out the window toward the water. As if it steadies her the same way it does me.

I tiptoe into the kitchen and, with both hands, place the thin glass on the marble counter next to the sink. Afraid to drop it and have it shatter on the tile floor.

"Did Mom hear anything?" I ask.

Mrs. Butler places her hand over the receiver. "What is it, Jess?"

"Did she hear anything?"

Mrs. Butler shakes her head and then speaks into the phone again. "I know this must be difficult. If there's anything I can do . . ."

Sam's followed me into the room, and he stands in front of the bay window. Beyond him, whitecaps dot the bay, and a single sailboat tacks with the wind.

Mrs. Butler hangs up.

She doesn't say my dad is injured.

But she doesn't say he isn't.

I'm glad, though, for what she does. Her strength comes through her hand and onto my shoulder the way my dad's does. She treats me like I am old enough for whatever the truth is. For whatever comes.

"Let's get you home," Mrs. Butler says.

"I call back seat." Sam dashes for the car before I can get out the door. He's trying to make me smile.

It works. Sort of.

I settle into the passenger seat and buckle up. Cinching the strap tighter, I feel it like the presence of Mrs. Butler's hand on my shoulder a few minutes ago.

As we drive by the PX, I crane my neck. A crowd has gathered. A security car, lights flashing, parks near the entrance. Word must be getting out.

I turn away. I don't want to think about the paper oleander flowers in the dark closet at the PX. Or the larger-than-life photo of Warda on the poster.

Mrs. Butler's cell phone rings, and she answers. "Yes," she says. And then, "No." A pause. "I see. I'll stop by." Neutral words.

After she says goodbye and cradles the phone in her lap, Mrs. Butler turns onto Monroe Street, the back way into the main housing area. In front of her a black car with government plates slows at the corner of Monroe and Madrid and flashes its turn signal.

My street.

It keeps going straight, though, as if changing its mind.

Pressure lifts off my chest.

"I should go see Meriwether."

Mrs. Butler turns at Madrid. "Home first," she says. "Your mother's worried about you."

I watch out the window as Mrs. Butler slows down at my house.

A strange car's parked out front. Not black, but navy blue with government tags. Two men in dress uniforms disappear into the front door.

I check the street number. 306.

My house.

Mrs. Butler parks behind the government car. I sit there. She squeezes my arm.

I force myself to get out.

If Mrs. Butler or Sam is talking to me, I can't hear either of them. The only thing I hear is the sound of my own pulse pounding in my ears. The way it would if I'd run all the way back. Just the *boom-boom-boom* of my heart and the strange swish of the sprinkler next door. A *shush-shush* followed by a metallic *rat-a-tat-tat*.

Like firecrackers going off.

 **SIX**

MRS. JOHNSON waves us inside. She must have been looking out the curtains, waiting for us to arrive. Had Mrs. Johnson seen the officers when they got out of the car? Did she tell Mom? Or did she wait until they were at the door?

"Girl, we were worried about you. Running out like that." Mrs. Johnson squeezes my arm. Her grip is stiff and awkward. Her face is red and splotchy, as if she's too hot. An unlit cigarette dangles from her lips. No one's allowed to smoke in our house.

"Mom?"

"Not so loud, Jess," Mrs. Johnson says. She nods over at the television. Cara's cross-legged in front of the screen. Too close. Watching some cartoons. She looks up, grins, and waves a toy dolphin at me.

"Come see," she says.

"I will, Cara. I just want to talk to Mom. Okay?" I speak to her gently, the way I would to someone I want to please.

Cara nods, her whole body moving. She goes back to the cartoons, and I slip into the kitchen.

Mom's at the table, holding two sheets of paper. The two officers sit there too, flanking her. It seems odd, them sitting in the kitchen and not in the living room. My computer's on one corner, unplugged in case of bad weather. Dad doesn't trust surge protectors. Cara's booster chair hangs on the wall where Dad installed a special shelf for it just Cara's height.

"It's one of the services available," one of the officers is saying.

"Mom, what's happening?"

"Now, Jess," Mrs. Johnson says, following me.

"It's okay, Libby." Mom's smile is tight, as if her skin is frozen.

"What's going on?" I ask.

"Jess, they found him. Daddy's alive," she says. "I'm going to meet him in Landstuhl."

"Landstuhl?" Germany, right? Dad's going to Germany from Afghanistan? Not to Florida?

"Why doesn't he just come home?" I ask.

"Master Sergeant Westmark will be coming home, miss. You can be sure of that," one of the officers says.

"Then why —"

"Not right away, Jess." Mom reaches for my hand. Her fingers are frozen too, like her face.

"What happened to Dad? How bad?" My voice rises at the edges the way Cara's does before a meltdown.

"Not so loud," Mrs. Johnson says. "We don't want to upset Cara." She says "we" when she means me — that I shouldn't upset my sister. She speaks in that tone that says I am just a kid barely older than Cara.

Get ahold of yourself, Jess. Make me proud.

Be calm. I'm counting on you.

Dad's words. I swallow and make myself nod. "Okay."

The two officers sit quietly at the table. Each one rests his hands on the surface, as if all the emotions in the room could be pressed as smooth as the wood.

"Daddy's injured, but he's not dead. He's going to be medically evacuated to Landstuhl." With each word, Mom's voice sounds a little stronger.

"How bad is it?" It must be bad, for them to send him all the way to Germany.

One of the officers speaks. "The reports aren't all in."

"He was in the Humvee?"

I remember the burned-out vehicle. No one could survive that.

Mom answers. "No, no, they think he was standing outside it. On the other side of the courtyard. The wall partially shielded him from the worst of the shrapnel and firebombing. It saved his life."

"So he's going to be okay?"

The cheek of one of the officers jerks.

"They're doing everything they can," Mom says.

Does she believe it?

"What does that mean?" I ask. "Doing everything" doesn't mean he'll be okay.

"They don't know the extent of his injuries. He's been unconscious since the incident." She calls it an incident. Not a bombing.

The officers' faces betray nothing.

"We'll be going, ma'am," one of them says, and they both stand.

"Thank you for coming," Mom says, and pushes herself up from her chair. "I appreciate all the information. And the flight coupons."

"I can show you out," Mrs. Johnson says.

Count on her to act like this is her house.

"That's okay, ma'am. We'll be fine showing ourselves out."

As the officers leave, I hear them greet Mrs. Butler.

I whirl around. She waits in the hallway, between the living room and the kitchen, where she must have been since we arrived. Behind her stands Sam with his hands stiff at his sides, like a soldier in formation on a hot parade ground.

Had they known?

Mom smiles. "Thank you for bringing Jess home. For being so good to her."

"I was happy to do anything I could. Jess is one of Sam's best friends. And we're all one family here." She says it like she means it. One family, regardless of whether officer or enlisted.

Mrs. Johnson busies herself with the coffeepot. She pours more coffee and offers a cup to Mrs. Butler, who takes it.

"Thank goodness he wasn't in the Humvee," Mrs. Johnson says.

But someone else must have been in the Humvee. That's what she means. "Who was in it?" I ask.

"We shouldn't be talking about that," Mrs. Johnson says. She yanks on the faucet and rinses out the coffeepot. Water spatters onto the counter. "We shouldn't speculate." She sounds like Mrs. Butler. But she can't stop there. She can't help it. "I'm sure there'll be an announcement."

And suddenly I know. Someone else *was* in the Humvee. No soldier could have gotten out of it alive. And what about the orphanage children? They were there too. "How about the children?"

"Who?" Mrs. Johnson frowns.

"From the orphanage? The girl in the photo?" *The one you don't want us to help?*

"No one's said anything about them."

"Then who?"

"Jess" — Mrs. Butler speaks softly, the way I talked to Cara — "they're just telling the families now."

Then I know. The phone call Mrs. Butler took on the drive home.

"Tell me."

Mrs. Johnson starts toward me.

"Don't." I hold out my hand like a stop sign. I look at Mrs. Butler. Before, she treated me like I was responsible.

"I'll tell you. You and Sam need to know," Mrs. Butler says.

Sam and I lock glances.

"Commander Butler called me while we were in the car. Two soldiers have been killed. Private Davis was one of them."

A face comes to my mind. A thin man from Arkansas. He liked to sing country-and-western music at the top of his lungs. He came with his wife and two little boys to the cookout my dad had before deployment.

Mrs. Butler continues. "Corporal Scott was the other casualty. She was killed while unloading the Humvee. It happened instantly."

She.

Corporal Scott.

The smoking frame of the Humvee in the distance on the television screen.

My memory shatters like a faulty satellite picture. Pixels break up and re-form.

The Humvee.

Mrs. Scott.

Meriwether's mother.

No.

The look in Mr. Scott's eyes, as if he knew. Before he could possibly have known.

Cara thunders into the kitchen in her pink princess pajamas. The embossed Cinderella image on the front has faded from too many times through the washing machine. But she won't wear anything else to sleep in. "Mom, come look. Mickey Mouse. Can we go?"

Mrs. Butler moves first. "Why don't you show me, Cara?" They walk out together, Cara tugging at Mrs. Butler's hand.

Meriwether's mother. Right now, three blocks away, Meriwether's world is coming apart. At the same time people exist whose lives go on and who are going to the Magic Kingdom.

A sob escapes into the room, and I don't know if it's mine or someone else's.

SEVEN

I FOLLOW MOM, Mrs. Butler, and Sam to the front door. Mrs. Butler exchanges phone numbers with Mom. Tells her whom to contact when she gets to Germany.

"You didn't know? Until just now?" I stand close to Sam. I have to know. *Duty, honor, country.* But duty is to your friends, too.

"No, I didn't know until you did." His eyes had locked on mine when his mom said "Corporal Scott."

"I have to go to Meriwether's," I say. We said we'd know if something happened to our parents in Afghanistan. We knew we'd know, by instinct. Like waking up in the morning and knowing it had rained overnight before looking out the window at the crape myrtles drooping over the sidewalk.

"Mom's going there now." Sam's eyes are dark brown, like the burrowing owl we found injured on the beach a month ago. We borrowed his mom's oven mitts to capture the bird so we could get it into a box and to an animal rescue organization. The owl hadn't fought us, though. Its dark eyes blinked slowly as if to say it knew what we were doing. That it was resigned to whatever was coming. Sam's eyes remind me of that owl's. As if he could see through the darkness.

But I don't know if he can see what's coming either.

"I'll call you later," he says.

"The orphanage. Find out what happened," I tell him.

"There'll have been casualties there."

Not Warda. Please.

"Maybe not," I say. "Maybe they were too far away."

"Jess, be real," he says. "You saw the explosion."

Saw the explosion? I still see it. Whenever I close my eyes. When I blink. It's as if the light has been imprinted on the surface of my eyeballs.

Mrs. Butler turns to me before she leaves. "Jess, while your mom's away, you're family."

I smile and nod. I don't trust myself to say anything. Not "Thank you" or "Don't go" or "Can I go with you to Meriwether's?"

Sam follows his mother out to their car.

Corporal Scott was carrying the boxes from the

Humvee. The school supplies we'd packaged — me and Meriwether and, sometimes, Sam. Pencils with smiley faces and pink ponies on blue backgrounds. Pen sets in all different colors. The plastic sharpeners we stuffed in empty corners of the boxes. Everything must have melted like crayons in the heat of the bombing. All the colors of the world.

As soon as the front door closes, Mom takes charge. It's as if she's woken from a month of sleeping. She has something to focus on. Something more to do than wait.

"Jess, get the rolling suitcase from the storage room," she says. "I need to pack. The plane's leaving at three."

Mrs. Johnson says, "I can help you organize."

"I'll do it," I say. Mrs. Johnson and I glare at each other. But Mom's already headed down the hallway. She misses our skirmish.

Mrs. Johnson turns away first, throwing up her hands. "I'll keep Cara out of mischief," she says.

I find the suitcase on top of the cooler that has my baby photos in it. Photos that belonged to me before I became a Westmark. I don't know what my last name was then. Mom said they kept Jess, that Jess had been my first name always. When I want to know, I can find out my old last name, she said. If I want to.

"Here, Mom. Here it is." I roll the large bag into my parents' bedroom. "What can I pack?"

I lift the bag onto the bed and unzip it. I run my fingers along the inside pocket and scoop out grains of sand. Tucked in one corner I find a folded bandanna the color of the gulf. I used the bag when Meriwether and I went to oceanography camp last summer. I can smell the warm salt air of our cabin, feet from the gulf. Hear Meriwether in the bottom bunk after I drew the short straw, her telling ghost stories after lights out. If I call her now, will she remember camp the way I do? Exactly down to the way we plopped a pat of soft butter into the middle of our bowl of grits in the canteen at breakfast? Suddenly, it matters that we have the same memories, that we remember the same scrunch of sand under our feet.

"Jess, are you listening?" Mom says.

"Sorry—"

"Pay attention," she says. "Try to find the deodorant samples. The new ones we just picked up. Check under the sink. Then I need you to get a piece of paper and write some things down."

I dash into Mom and Dad's bathroom and fling open the cabinet. Plastic bins hold mountains of mini bottles of shampoo and conditioner, travel-size tubes of toothpaste.

I pack Mom's toiletries and zip the bag shut.

"Okay, what else?"

Mom stands in front of Dad's side of their closet. She runs her hands along a few of his shirts.

"I'll need those cotton pants, and the hooded jacket. Airplanes are always too cold."

"I know where they are." Mom stores extra clothes in the hall closet, tiny as it is. She manages to get our cold-weather things into it. Not that we need them often.

I roll the pants and set them next to the suitcase. I leave the hoodie out for her carry-on bag.

"Get some notepaper, Jess."

I run to the kitchen and grab a notebook and a pen. When I fly through the living room, I hear Mrs. Johnson reading Cara's favorite storybook about the caribou.

Mom's rolling her pajamas when I get back to the bedroom.

"How long?" I ask her.

"I don't know. I'm planning for two weeks. It could be longer."

"Why don't I go with you?" I could help out. Stay with Dad while she gets some sleep.

Mom tries on a pair of loafers, then pitches them back into the closet.

"I could help," I repeat.

She stuffs a pair of sandals into a liner pocket of the suitcase. "I need you to stay here."

She had heard me.

"With Cara," she says. "She needs you here. I need you here. You're the big sister."

"But—"

Mom reaches over and puts her hand on mine. "I'm counting on you. Just like your dad is."

I nod.

"Jess, you take notes. I'll get the last things out of the cabinet." She disappears into the bathroom. The cabinet door creaks open again. "Okay. One, you have to watch Cara every time you go to the pool with her. You know she isn't afraid of anything. I warned Libby, but you need to keep an eye out."

She wants me to write that down?

"But, Mom—"

"Two. No chocolate for Cara. She gets sick."

And cranky. "I know."

"Are you writing this down?"

I scrawl out the directions so far. "Yes."

"The bills. I think they're paid up. But I need you to look for them. Get the mail every day and open anything that looks official. If anything is due soon, let Mrs. Johnson know. We'll figure out what to do if I'm not back soon enough."

"It's okay, Mom. I'm sure the army will help."

"They don't pay the bills, Jess." Mom throws a few more things into the suitcase and rips the zipper closed. "Heaven knows they don't do that." She lifts the bag upright onto the floor.

"I want you to keep up your routine, Jess. Go to the beach. Go to the pool. Get ready for camp." But nothing's routine, I want to tell her. I do those things with Meriwether.

I open my mouth to say something, but Mom's still talking.

"Chores, too. You do your own laundry. Help Mrs. Johnson with the housework."

I hold the pencil in midair. "Mrs. Johnson?"

Mom makes a funny look with her mouth.

"I asked Libby to stay with you while I'm gone."

My mouth drops open. "But why does she have to stay here?"

I don't want her hovering over me. She already feels too much at home here. What will she do next? Sleep in my parents' bedroom?

"Come on, Jess. You can't stay here alone with Cara."

"I —" Before I can say anything else, Cara bursts into the room and jumps onto Mom's bed. Into the things she's set aside to go into her carry-on.

"Cara!" I wrestle her off the bed, and her face goes pink, then red. Big tears loom on the edges of her lashes.

"There you are." Mrs. Johnson stands at the bedroom door. "I know a little princess who wants a treat." She holds a package of Popsicles in her hands.

Cara stops pouting and slips off the bed, running

after Mrs. Johnson, who heads back to the kitchen, where she makes sandwiches.

Just after the lunch that no one eats, a horn honks outside.

The cab's here.

Mom rolls the bag into the living room. "I want to check my purse first. Passport, boarding pass. Wallet." The military support unit had arranged Mom's flights. "I'm going to tell Cara."

While Mom's in the kitchen, I run into my bedroom and dig for the envelope containing the letter I wrote to her in Ms. Rivera's class before deployment. The one I hadn't given her. Because it seemed so silly then to write a letter to someone who wasn't going anywhere, not like Dad. I'd told her how much I missed Dad's whistling reveille. How Dad had told me he bought her perfume he spent half a day's pay on when they were just married. I grab a chocolate bar, too, from my drawer that's too high for Cara to reach. I slip them both into Mom's carry-on just as she's heading for the door.

"They don't have American chocolate over there." I make an excuse for why I'm slipping something into her bag.

"Of course they do," Mrs. Johnson says. "You can even get Hershey's. Though who wants milk chocolate when you can get the best dark chocolate in the world?"

Mom's holding Cara in her arms.

"It's okay. Jess knows I prefer milk chocolate." Mom winks at me, and I hug her hard, my arms around both her and Cara.

Mom nods at Mrs. Johnson and passes Cara to her without making a big production. Cara hasn't figured it all out yet. I see the tears in Mom's eyes, though, as she leaves.

The rollaway bag clatters over the seams in the driveway as Mom makes her way toward the waiting cab and climbs in.

I watch the car until it turns at the end of the street and disappears.

Only then do I notice Mom's gardenia blooming white by the steps, the blossoms like ghosts. The sweet scent too strong to bear.

EIGHT

AFTER MOM leaves, we wander around like we're in a stranger's house. Eventually, we gather in the kitchen, even Mrs. Johnson. I'm not sure why. Maybe it's because that was where we heard the official news. When we'd all been together.

I wash out the coffee cups from earlier. Mom's, Mrs. Johnson's, and Mrs. Butler's. I scrub the counter, too, where the cups have left faint brown rings. I bear down hard with the sponge.

"I'm just going over to grab a few things from my house," Mrs. Johnson says. "I'll be right back. Keep an eye on Cara."

I squint at her. Does she think I need her to tell me to take care of Cara? I've been taking care of Cara since she was just a baby. No one except Mom and Dad has ever been as careful about Cara as I am.

Cara nibbles peanut butter cookies at the kitchen table. Mrs. Johnson told her she could have two before dinner. She eats both of them around the edge like a bunny chewing a carrot, making them last as long as possible. If Mom were here, she'd tell Cara to cut it out and eat them like a little girl should. But I don't say anything. I let her eat them the way she wants.

The door to the carport clicks shut behind Mrs. Johnson. I dry the cups and put them away. I take in a deep breath and let it out. I count to ten, to make sure she's gone. Then I wipe my hands on the dishtowel and dial Meriwether's number on the phone.

The spaces between the rings stretch out longer than usual. Four rings, and still no answer. The machine message comes on. Will Meriwether pick up as soon as I say my name?

The answering-machine voice comes over the phone. It's Meriwether's mother's voice asking the caller to leave a message and a number at the tone. I almost drop the receiver. When the machine beeps, for a moment nothing comes out of my mouth. Then, in a rush, "Meriwether, it's me, Jess. I'm so sorry. Please call me."

I hang up.

The door to the carport opens.

Mrs. Johnson pushes inside. Her carpetbag purse bounces against her rib cage, and she hauls a box of frozen pizza.

Mrs. Johnson speaks to Cara in a tempting voice like a villainess in a Disney movie. "Piz-za!"

Cara grins. "Pizza!" Peanut butter cookie crumbs rim her mouth.

Traitor. Somehow Mrs. Johnson knows the only food group Cara likes besides Popsicles and cookies is pizza.

"Put the oven on, Jess. Four hundred fifty degrees." I turn back to the stove and jerk the dial over to the right setting. Mom's not even been gone an hour, and it feels like forever.

When will Meriwether call me back?

The telephone rings, and my feet hit the bedroom floor. Pale light glows around the blinds. Not as bright as yesterday. I run for the phone in the living room and catch it before it rings a second time.

I squint at the clock. Seven in the morning.

"Mom?"

"Jess?"

"Hi, Mom," I say. Her voice sounds slow, but maybe she's tired. Or maybe it's just the long-distance satellite phone distorting her voice. I press my hand over my other ear to hear her better. "How's Dad?"

There's a delay in the line. My voice echoes across the miles, as if each syllable has to cross the Atlantic Ocean separately.

Mrs. Johnson staggers into the room — she *is* sleeping in my parents' bed — her hair unbrushed. Her eyebrows form questions I want to ignore, but I nod before I look away.

"It's hard to hear you," Mom says. "I saw your dad for a few minutes when I got in. He's still unconscious, though. He hasn't been awake since the attacks."

Dad doesn't know he's in Germany; he doesn't know they flew him from Afghanistan on a medevac plane. Maybe he doesn't even know that Meriwether's mother and Private Davis are dead. I blink and wonder whether inside his head he's trapped in a whiteout that blots out everything.

"Why can't they wake him up?" I wind the cord in my hand.

"They're keeping him sedated. On purpose. He's going back into surgery today."

"For what?"

"Some shrapnel in his left eye. They're concerned about both of his eyes. He has a concussion, too. And neck injuries. Because of where he was standing, most of his injuries are upper body. Is Libby there?"

"Yes," I say, but I don't let go of the phone. "When will they know something?"

"I don't know, Jess. It could be another day or two," Mom says. She pauses. "I found your note, Jess. Thank you. You don't know how much that means to me."

I press my eyelids together hard. But I'm not going to cry. Not here. Not in front of Mrs. Johnson. Not where Mom can hear me. *Be strong for me, Jess.* That's what Dad would say.

"Here's Mrs. Johnson." I pass the phone over.

Mrs. Johnson says "Hello" and then waits, listening. "Oh, we're doing fine. Had a little pizza last night." This time she's the one who doesn't meet my eyes. Mrs. Johnson doesn't tell Mom what a pain Cara became last night. Maybe it was all the sugar from the Popsicle and the cookies. Maybe it was Mom going away and Cara not really understanding. But when we finally got her to sleep — after I read her the caribou story again — Mrs. Johnson and I had also collapsed, exhausted. Mrs. Johnson doesn't tell Mom any of this.

Is Mom doing the same thing on the other end of the phone? Telling us only part of the story so we won't worry?

The morning light comes through the kitchen window. Patchy fog drapes over the backyard and our neighbor's bamboo fence.

"Sure, I'll make sure she does," Mrs. Johnson says, nodding toward me.

What? What's Mom telling her?

"What's that?" Mrs. Johnson's voice rises, as if there's some background noise. She covers her other ear the way I did. "Let us know. And get some rest, you hear?"

"Wait." I grab for the phone as Mrs. Johnson hangs up the receiver. "Hello?"

But the line's dead.

"I wasn't finished talking to Mom."

"I'm sorry, your mother had to go. One of the doctors came in to talk to her. You don't keep them waiting. Your dad's going in for more surgery."

"What did you mean — 'make sure she does'?" I ask.

"Your mother said that I need to make sure you get out of the house and don't stay stuck here like some tick on a dog. Worrying about things. I can handle Cara."

I fold my arms. Handling Cara had taken both of us last night.

"I know what you're thinking," Mrs. Johnson says. "I'm figuring that child out. She's like my old cat, Horace. I could open five cans of cat food before His Highness would eat one. Drat it all if that cat sometimes didn't go back and pick the very first can I'd opened. After all that."

"What'd you do?" I ask, despite everything.

"I got smarter, that's what. I opened two at once and gave him a little of both. Put the rest away and left the room. That was that. The old cat just wanted me crooning over him. Sometimes you have to step back."

I nod.

"Okay, breakfast, and then I want you out of the house," Mrs. Johnson says. She opens the refrigerator door and retrieves eggs. "You can help by scrambling these."

I press my lips together. She's ordering me around again, and we haven't even survived twenty-four hours together yet. How many more days before Mom and Dad come home?

"Do we wake Cara up?" she asks me.

"Let her sleep," I say, not ready to deal with my sister.

"My thoughts exactly," Mrs. Johnson says, getting out two plates and silverware and setting the table.

I crack the eggs into a bowl and whisk in some milk the way Dad does. Then I beat the mixture until it's golden yellow.

As soon as breakfast's over, I know what I have to do. Where I have to go.

NINE

I STAND IN front of Meriwether's house, trying to convince myself to walk up the sidewalk and knock. The sun has pushed the fog out, leaving every surface covered in a thin layer of dampness, as if the world is waking up sweaty from a bad dream. Small American flags line the driveway. A wreath of red, white, and blue ribbons hangs from the door. Curtains on windows flanking the door remain closed.

The house looks as if no one's home. Maybe Meriwether and her dad are sleeping in. Maybe they went away.

From the back of their house, though, I hear a sound. At first I can't tell what it is. But it's not like someone breaking in or anything. In fact, it sounds more like yard work.

Yard work?

I tiptoe down the driveway. The gate of the carport is unlocked, and the gate hangs open. I walk through and into the backyard.

For a moment seeing the backyard takes away my breath. Meriwether's mother had turned the far corner of the yard into a magical area, with tiny white lights strung into dwarf trees. Last summer I helped them dig a hole large enough for a plastic pond, complete with fountain and some goldfish they'd bought on sale. Last time I was over, though, only two flickers of orange could be seen hiding in the dark green watercress. A heron had eaten the rest of the fish, but Meriwether's mother, from her base in Afghanistan, made us promise her we wouldn't do anything to scare away the heron.

And so we hadn't.

Now I can hear a faint gurgle of water from the fountain.

That, and digging.

In the sunny part of the yard, Meriwether and I had helped Mrs. Scott plant day lilies in every color and variety. Bright yellow, scarlet with lemon stripes down their centers, salmon pink ones with petals dusted in diamonds. Single and double petals, straight-edged and fringed ones. Like she had, I loved them all — not for their scent, because these didn't have much. But for the way the flowers opened in the morning when the sun came out and then closed up at night. I told Mrs. Scott it was so they could dream. I'd turned red when I said that, when we stood out in the yard, hot and sweaty after planting a new grouping, because it had seemed silly when I said it out loud. But Mrs. Scott said she'd always think of day lilies that way. That they dream like we do.

This past year the day lilies have filled in. They've grown tall and thick. Flowered stalks reach for the sky.

In the middle of them, Meriwether kneels.

With a shovel in her hand.

"Meriwether?"

She jerks around. Her T-shirt's soaked through, and tendrils of her hair have escaped her ponytail clip. They curl against her damp neck and upper arms, like swirls of grass after a heavy rain.

"Go away," she says.

The shovel is caked with dirt. Clumps of day lilies, wilting, lie on their sides on the lawn. Ripped like weeds from the earth.

"Stop!" She's tearing them up. Destroying her mother's garden. "What are you doing? Don't kill them."

When I say the word "kill," Meriwether drops the clump from her hands. She puts a dirty hand to her forehead as if she has a headache.

The word "kill" echoes back and forth between us.

I cover my mouth, not trusting the right words to come out.

"I'm not killing them. I'm transplanting them." Meriwether says each word with force, as if I'm an idiot.

"Oh," I say. "Sorry, it just looked . . ."

Meriwether sits back. She sprays some water from the hose onto the exposed roots.

"Where?" I ask.

"South Carolina. Maybe. Whenever we leave, I'm not abandoning these flowers. Mom loved them."

"What's in South Carolina?" I should know, but I can't remember.

"My grandparents." Meriwether's almost yelling at me. "They live in Charleston. Remember?"

That's right. Mrs. Scott had talked about the salt marshes and the herons of the low country, the red-winged blackbirds that nested in the marshes.

"I'm sorry, Meriwether." I stand a few feet from her, and I don't know what to do. Best friends hug each other, don't they? Best friends know without saying anything what to do. "You're coming back, right?"

My question hangs there. Meriwether looks away. She digs out another clump of day lilies and lays them in the shade. She sprays them with water.

"I can help you," I say.

"I don't want your help."

She says it like she's mad at me.

"Are you moving?" I ask. "Is that why?"

"Yes, we're moving. Dad says he can't stay here."

"When?"

"A few weeks. As soon as they can schedule the movers. But tomorrow night we're flying to Dover. We'll be back. For the funeral." Meriwether stabs the shovel into the soft ground where the hose has dripped.

I reach for the hose. "I can help. Really. Please." I need to help. I need to do something. *Please.*

Meriwether pushes it away from me. "No, Jess. I don't want your help."

"Why?"

Meriwether doesn't answer. Wiping her hands on the lawn, she stands and gathers plants into her arms, moving toward the garage.

I follow her.

"Why?"

Meriwether wraps the roots in burlap and stashes them in a bucket. She stomps into the house, leaving a track of muddy footprints. Mrs. Scott would make her take off her dirty shoes by the back door and use the hose to rinse them off.

"Meriwether."

It's as if she's gone deaf.

She steps into the kitchen. The light comes in the

window and makes the azure tiles glow like the gulf. "Not blue," Mrs. Scott said. "Azure." It's a word that conjures up Greek islands and tropical drinks. "Virgin drinks, of course," she'd say, and laugh, as if it were a joke. A joke that she told when they had company. Whenever her mother would say "virgin," Meriwether exhaled in a puff of embarrassment.

Meriwether washes her hands in the sink. Trickles of dirty water drip along the counter. I ache to wipe them away like the rings from yesterday's coffee cups at home.

Everything in the house reminds me of Mrs. Scott, and I don't know how Meriwether stands it. I'd be half-crazy.

Maybe that's what's wrong.

Meriwether's shut everything out. Become like a zombie because it's too hard otherwise. She brushes past me, moving her shoulder in an exaggerated way, as if to show she won't touch me. Her room is down the hall.

"Meriwether—" I reach for her.

"Don't." Meriwether jerks back. She retreats into her room. On the bed, her back against the wall, she barricades herself with pillows. I stand at the door. That's another thing I always loved about Meriwether's house—enough throw pillows to stack to the ceiling. In all colors. Some striped, some polka dotted. A riot of color, as if Mrs. Scott's day lily garden had been transplanted indoors.

"I called as soon as — I mean, I called. Last night. I wanted to tell you in person. I'm so sorry," I say. "What can I do to help?"

"Do?" Meriwether's red-rimmed eyes squint. "You can't do anything."

"Why don't we go outside? Walk to the beach?" I can't stand it in the house anymore. Everything reminds me of Mrs. Scott, and I can't breathe. Because I love her too.

On the beach, I can breathe, and I can cry and taste the salt on my cheeks as though it's just ocean spray.

"The beach?" Meriwether's voice accuses me, as if I've suggested we put on bikinis and go to a party.

"I'm really sorry."

"You should be." Meriwether grabs another pillow, pressing it against her stomach as if to hold herself together.

I touch the door to steady myself. The floor moves underneath me like the deck of a boat.

"If it weren't for you, my mom wouldn't have been at that stupid orphanage in the first place. I didn't even want to help you. Remember?" Meriwether flings words at me like acid spray.

I nod the way a marionette does when a puppeteer yanks a string. The *orphanage.* The way she says it stabs me. Meriwether's face is blotchy.

"Every day since school's been out, I've gotten up to sit at that stupid booth with you and ask people for money for school supplies. I don't even like mornings. My mom couldn't believe I was getting up. She told me she thought it was *great*. That maybe I was finally an army brat after all."

My brain feels thick as felt.

"And you know what else?"

Now I am the one unable to talk. Unsure of what comes next. I am sinking, pulled down by undertow in the gulf, and there's no lifeguard on duty to save me. I see myself sucked farther down and away from shore. I can't fight it.

"I never said this before because I didn't want to hurt your feelings. But oleander, Jess? That's the stupidest name I ever heard of. Oleander is poisonous. Don't you know that?"

I nodded. Every summer the local news carries stories about people who poison themselves accidentally by inhaling oleander fumes from a beach bonfire. Or people who use oleander twigs to roast hot dogs. But what had drawn me was the photo of the oleander growing next to the orphanage, all the way in Afghanistan. It bonded us all together — Warda, Dad, and me. Poisonous, yes, but in its own way, oleander is beautiful, and it grows in places that more delicate plants can't.

"You knew and you wanted to use the name anyway?"

"Yes, I —"

"Just go. Get out."

Her words pummel my body.

"Okay," I say. "I'll go. If you really want me to." I wait, hoping Meriwether will say something else.

She just sits there, protected by her pillows.

"I didn't know this would happen. I love your mom too." I don't tell her my dad's condition, how he might still die.

I slip out and close the door behind me. I feel my heart stabbed through like an insect pinned to a board.

Outside, my eyes blurry, I walk past the flower beds. Where Meriwether removed the day lilies, a bare spot of earth lies exposed, a gaping wound.

TEN

THIS TIME of the day, heat builds over land. Later, an afternoon thunderstorm will crackle, and rain will pour down out of the sky as if a dam holding it back has given way. But right now it's just hot and sticky, and the sunlight hurts my eyes. I walk to the beach anyway.

Away from Meriwether's house. Away from the pond with its two frightened goldfish and the flower bed that looks like a war zone. And my best friend who says her mother wouldn't have been at the orphanage that morning except for me.

When the news of the bombing broke, I only thought about Dad. It hadn't come to my mind that Meriwether's mother might be hurt, or that others I knew would be killed.

No, it was Dad and the orphanage I thought about

first. And Warda. And, if she's alive, whether her eyes now hold more pain in them than I'd already seen in the photos. The newscasters don't report on the orphanage. Maybe they think there's no story in that here.

I follow the beach road until it curves like the scar created by the water. Then I slip off my flip-flops and run onto the sand, toward the gulf. The whiteness of the sun reflecting off the beach burns my eyes.

Because of Operation Oleander.

Everything is whiteness. Hot whiteness.

I dash toward the surf, but I don't dive in. *Don't swim alone,* my dad's voice reminds me. Instead I run through the surf, kicking up water and sand. Water courses down my legs. One wave surges toward me, and water splashes up to my thighs. The edges of my shorts turn damp. Later they'll dry stiff from all the salt water.

This morning there's no one here except for one old man. He wears a faded green army cap and fishes in the surf. I've seen him before. I think he's retired. He's so dark and wrinkled that it's as if he's turned to seaweed that washes up on the sand at high tide.

The sun's overhead. I keep running. My feet push off. Digging into the wet sand, trying to release myself, tugging against the wet sand pulling me down, holding me back.

I fight. Push harder. Run faster.

And then I am finally flying, tripping, and soaring until I dive into the water.

When you're in it, water has a sound of its own. I am underneath, and it washes over me. Close my eyes because it stings. But I hear the gush of it, the gurgle all around me, almost as if the gulf is breathing. I listen to it gather and swell toward land.

I hold my breath until my chest aches.

Then I bellow out of the water like a breaching whale, gasping for air.

Beyond the point, the old man who's fishing raises his hat to wave at me. He's checking on me. He must think I'm crazy or drowning.

I am both.

In the water, no one can see my tears.

In the water, I am not even sure I am crying.

I wave back once and trudge out of the surf so he doesn't think I need rescuing. Water streams down my face and my neck, into the folds of my T-shirt, my shorts. I squeeze out my hair and find my flip-flops in the white, hot sand.

By the time I get home, I am half-dry and my skin itches with salt.

In the time I've been gone, someone has tied red, white, and blue ribbons to the front porch of our house. A couple of smaller ribbons trim the branches of the gardenia like ornaments.

For the first time, our house appears different from others on the block. It looks marked. Like Meriwether's house.

"There you are," Mrs. Johnson says when I squish into the kitchen. She's holding the lid of a casserole dish, and steam billows out into the air like a cloud from a genie's lamp. Steam fogs the window and her glasses. She sets the lid down. "You didn't drown — that's obvious. What did you do?"

At least she didn't ream me out the way Dad would have.

"I went to Meriwether's house."

Her eyebrows wrinkle. "She doesn't have a pool."

"I went to the beach. After." I take a deep breath. "I had to take a walk." I hold in my stomach as if she might scold me. Or drill me like a master sergeant for details about what happened with Meriwether.

She just nods.

"Look. Some women from the auxiliary dropped by with food for dinner. People are starting to hear about your dad, and your mom over in Germany. This is beef stroganoff. Enough sour cream to clog my arteries, but it sure smells good."

I breathe in, but the baked noodles don't smell like

anything. My nose still holds the sea and the scent of gardenias.

"Isn't that nice of them?" Mrs. Johnson asks.

"I'm not hungry." I don't understand why people bring food when bad things happen. I don't want to eat.

Mrs. Johnson cocks her head to one side.

"It's nice of people to reach out in ways they can. And I'm not going to let you starve. What do you think your mom would do if she comes home and you're thin as a rail? You're practically that now."

Meriwether told me I was cheerleader thin. She meant it as a compliment. Back before deployment, I'd gone shopping for bathing suits with her and her mom. Mrs. Scott wanted to do everything to get Meriwether ready for the months she wouldn't be here. I found two suits — I only had money for one, and I had to turn over every single wrinkled dollar bill I had — but Meriwether hadn't found one that flattered her body.

She isn't fat, but she has high school girl curves already. Boys from high school are already following her with their gazes at the pool or the beach. If a car drives by with a teenage boy at the wheel, it slows down and slinks by when I'm with Meriwether. Never when I'm by myself, which is okay with me.

Mrs. Johnson's standing there waiting for an answer.

What was the question?

"I'll eat later," I say, hoping that's what she wants to hear.

"Deal." She reaches for a serving spoon. "Cara's playing in your bedroom. Have you written your dad a note?"

My hand grasps the back of the spindle chair at the kitchen table. "No. Not yet." What do I tell him? "I will later."

Her look says it all. That I should do it now.

"I think I'll go set up the table," I say. "At the PX." I want to say *we,* but I know there is no we. Meriwether blames Operation Oleander for interfering with her summer plans to get Caden's attention. And now this. As for Sam, well, I can guess what he thinks.

"You think you ought to be doing that? Earth to Jess, didn't you hear what happened? They bombed our troops," Mrs. Johnson says. She says it as if I'm deaf from the explosion.

But I do hear. I don't know the answer. I've never thought about what we would do if the orphanage were damaged, or how we'd get supplies there. But I can't think about that now. I have to keep going until I know what happened for sure.

"I know what happened. But they bombed the orphanage, too. That's what the Taliban want us to do. They want us to quit and let things go back the way they were. When girls couldn't go to school. They want us to give up."

I can't do that.

"Yes, they want us to give up. Two of our own dead, and one wounded. Sounds like they might get what they want," Mrs. Johnson says. "For now. Trust me — no one on this post is going to want to be reminded about that orphanage. Not right now."

"I can't quit." *Duty, honor, country.* Dad wouldn't want me to give up because of violence. That's what people do when they're not tough enough. When they let things knock them off track and lose sight of what they believe in. Right? He's right, isn't he?

Mrs. Johnson's cheek twitches, and she snaps the lid back on the stroganoff. "Flags are half-mast on post. You ought to give it a rest."

"Is that an order?"

"Jess — "

But I plug in my earbuds. I'm no longer listening to her.

ELEVEN

I SHOWER AND change clothes. Mrs. Johnson left a note saying she and Cara have gone for ice cream, and she'll bring me a cone.

A peace offering?

I scribble out a note that I'm at the PX.

When I get there, the whole place is crowded. People stream in and out. Little kids and high schoolers congregate at the far end of the complex near the rec center. On the far end, there's also a basketball court.

The table's still in the hallway. Empty cups and candy wrappers have been left on top, so I clean it off. Then I unlock the closet and get our supplies. First I cover the table with the cloth and Mrs. Scott's baskets. I flatten out the wrinkles in the blue linen with my palms and sort the snacks the way Meriwether would have. Potato chips and pretzels in separate baskets.

Everything's out, except for the sodas. When I finally prop the poster of Warda on the metal frame, it wobbles. I hold my breath, ease it over until it balances. Then I wipe my palms on my shorts.

I take one of the extra posters and tape it to the sliding glass doors in front of the PX. To make sure everyone sees it.

A soldier walking into the building detours around me. He frowns. Whether at me or the poster I'm not sure. I press harder on the glass, getting the edges of the poster smooth. Trying to get the air bubbles out from underneath the tape.

Behind me, I hear voices at the table. A man in uniform says to a woman with him, "That's Master Sergeant Westmark in that photo." They study the picture. "We ought to be giving money for *him*."

Maybe I'm wrong to be here.

But I can't forget about the orphanage. It's why we were here. Why Dad was there when the bomb went off.

The woman lays the poster on the table.

"Come on, honey." She touches the man's arm.

I force myself to smile. Stepping closer, I make myself speak up. "Can I tell you anything about the orphanage?"

The woman blushes, but she doesn't put the poster back where it belongs.

"I just don't think we should play on people's emotions right now. To earn money for charity, or for anything else. It's like those animal-shelter ads — they try to break your heart." The woman folds her arms.

"It's not the orphans' fault. Since the bombing, they need us more than ever."

The woman's cheeks go a deeper red. "I'm sure they need lots of things. Things we can't do for them. But what about our own soldiers? How about this Master Sergeant Westmark? He's gravely wounded in Germany."

"Yes, he is," I hear myself say.

"We should focus on him." She twists the wedding band on her hand.

"Yes, well, he's my dad. I think he'd want me to continue." Dad never gives up. When he and Mom wanted to have children and they couldn't, they looked into adoption. Dad said it took them years to find a child, the right child.

If they'd given up, I wouldn't be here.

The woman's face drains of color. "I'm — I'm sorry," she says, and walks away, weaving her way between people coming from the PX with piled-high grocery carts. The soldier calls after her to wait for him.

I squeeze my eyes shut.

Everything I touch is going wrong. Dad, Meriwether, Operation Oleander.

I stab the paper flowers into the vase.

"Those are pretty," a voice says.

The voice belongs to a girl I've seen before. She arrived new at school just before it ended. Her white-blond hair is clipped on one side with yellow and green barrettes. Evie or Aria or something like that.

"Thanks." I try to keep my voice even and not make eye contact.

Looking down, I see her toenails painted bright green and yellow, too, like parrots' wings.

"Who's that?" the girl asks.

Why doesn't she leave?

I study the poster with its collage of photos the way a stranger would. "An orphan."

Just like millions in the world. Like I was once.

"Does she have a name?"

"Does it matter?" I ask.

The girl steps back as if I've yelled at her. She is thin and frail, and I am suddenly mean.

"She's just an Afghan orphan," I say.

I slash at the baskets with my hands, and they fly off the table. Packages of chips and pretzels skitter across the floor like insects looking for a place to hide.

The girl with the painted toenails flees.

I grab the paper oleanders from the vase with my bare hands, the way Meriwether uprooted day lilies. I grip them hard in both fists, ready to tear them into tiny bits of confetti. Like leftover fireworks.

But I can't.

I pull them to my chest and cradle them. The faint, sweet smell of real oleander crushes into my T-shirt.

"Jess!"

Sam stands in front of me, his eyes wide. Like he doesn't know me.

"Don't," he says. In his hand he holds out the poster I'd taped to the glass doors. "What's going on?"

"I want to keep the operation going," I say, still hugging the paper flowers.

Strangers walk by the table, Sam and me on opposite sides of it, and they don't stop. They pretend nothing is happening.

"I called your house. Mrs. Johnson said you'd left a note while she was out, that you'd be here." He says it like it's a crime.

"Oh, so you're finally here to help me?" I glare at him.

"I'll help you put stuff away." His voice is calm, the way I talk to Cara when she's in super meltdown.

"Maybe I don't want to put it all away." I slap the paper flowers onto the table, and they make a faint snapping sound. Not nearly loud enough. I grab for a basket that's upended on the floor.

Two soldiers walk close by. One cranes his neck and scans the poster that lies flat on the table. He shakes his head.

"What are you looking at?" I dare him to answer me back. He marches away with the other soldier. The tips of his ears turn pink.

"Come on, Jess. It's too soon." Sam moves closer. He lowers his voice. "Let's go talk somewhere."

That's too funny. Sam wants to talk to me, and I want to talk to Meriwether.

"*Now* you want to talk about Operation Oleander?"

"Seriously, Jess." Sam corrals the bags of chips back into a storage box under the table.

"Why'd you take the poster down?" The anger sparks in me like a fuse being lit under bottle rockets.

"Because we never had permission to do anything but the table. A discreet in-kind charitable drive." He says the last four words like he's reading from a military manual.

I can't believe it. "We need permission to put something in the window glass at the PX?"

"Yes," he says. "It's not my fault. I don't make the rules."

Of course the military would have some rule about

whether posters could be posted. That would be just like the army. But I don't want to hear it. Not now.

I snatch snacks out of Sam's hands and start restocking the baskets.

"Don't you know what they're saying?" Sam asks. "Locals in Kabul are blaming our soldiers for the bombing."

"No." I shake my head. "It's not true."

"Some people believe it."

"Exactly. That's why we have to keep going."

"People will think you're disrespecting Corporal Scott and Private Davis. They'll say you're doing this for yourself. To get attention."

"How can you say that? Is that what you think I'm doing?"

He shakes his head.

"For my own reasons? Isn't doing something for others a good thing?"

"I'm sorry I said that, Jess," Sam says. "But you have to know what people over in Afghanistan are thinking. It's too soon to go back to this. That's all I mean. This isn't like Toby."

Toby was a boy from our class last year who had leukemia. The classes organized teams to collect pop tabs to help out with his medical bills. Sam, Meriwether, and I were a team. We collected the most of any team; that's how good we were. We won free tickets to Calypso Crazy Golf and all-you-can-eat pizza.

"I know that."

"Do you? Really?" Sam asks. "Because this is about Afghanistan. It's about a war. It's more than some make-believe operation."

In front of my eyes, fireworks flash.

"You don't have to tell me, Sam Butler, about soldiers in Afghanistan. Your dad isn't there. Mine is. Or he was. Now he's in a hospital in Germany."

Sam flinches, then shifts his weight from one foot to the other, as if he isn't sure whether to go or stay.

His voice lowers.

"I'm just saying they have a point. This charity thing — okay, we did it. Some good — maybe — came from it. But look what's happened. Two soldiers died. Your dad's wounded. It isn't just about orphaned kids over there. It's about American soldiers, too. What about them? What about your dad? What if this is *our* fault?"

Our fault.

My head spins, crazy, like some roller-coaster ride that flips you upside down halfway through.

"Don't you mean *my* fault?"

"Jess — "

"Just go."

Sam nods. "I didn't come to fight. There's a candlelight service tonight. My church. I wanted you to come with us."

I've been to Sam's church before. Church of the Nativity. It's Catholic, and it's nothing like the plain old meeting space for the Bible church we sometimes attend. But inside the stucco walls with the wooden beams, the crucifix, which I won't let myself stare at, I have always been comforted.

Lots of people from the post will go. The whole of Clementine will be drawn together tonight. Maybe Meriwether and her dad will go.

"Maybe," I say, barely above a whisper. I won't commit.

"I'll wait for you outside the church," Sam says. He lays the poster from the sliding glass doors on the tabletop, the pieces of tape folded back, neatly.

With army precision.

TWELVE

S AM'S WAITING by the door like he said he would be,
even though I'm almost late. Mrs. Johnson insisted
on driving me, and then she got stuck in traffic. Sam hands
me a candle that sits inside a plastic holder to catch any
wax that falls. So we don't burn our fingers. I inhale, but
the candle doesn't have a scent, not beeswax or perfume.
Not even plastic. It's odorless.

Inside the church even the little children are quiet.
That's what impresses me when we first walk in. Then it's
the coolness of the sanctuary on my skin, and I think of
that word. *Sanctuary*. A place of safety, a refuge.

The lights are low enough so everyone has to slow
down. Our eyes adjust from the brightness outside. The
crucifix hangs in front, and the scenes along the wall are
carved in relief. Once, Sam walked me through the Sta-

tions of the Cross. I don't remember all the steps. But closest to us is the figure of Christ carrying his own cross. He staggers under the weight.

Sam genuflects and enters a pew near the back that's not yet full. I don't bend my knees, but I lower my eyes as I follow him. In the row in front of us are other students from school. They don't look back.

I turn my head looking for Meriwether or her dad, but I don't see them.

Almost every pew is filled, and people stand along the back in neat rows. Father Killen leads everyone in prayer, and Sam points me to the preselected list of hymns and prayers on the back of the paper flyer.

An usher lights the candle of the first person in every row. Then each person shares it with the next person. When the time comes, I tip the wick of my candle into the elderly woman's to my right. Her freckled hand shakes, and I hold my breath, afraid the flame will go out. But the wick catches. Shielding the candle from the draft of my own movement, I turn to my left and pass the light to Sam. Soon the only light in the sanctuary comes from flickering candles. Pure light, and then voices fill the room in song.

This isn't a regular mass, but Father Killen speaks of coming together, of remembrance, mystery, pain. Of healing. Of prayer. Mostly, though, we are singing. "Amazing

Grace" I know. But also "Holy, Holy, Holy" and "Peace Is Flowing Like a River."

When it's over, I find myself separated from Sam as we walk out. I'm going through the door, and suddenly, I'm standing next to Father Killen as he greets everyone leaving through the main entrance.

I shake his hand like the person before me did. I expect his hand to be cold, but it's warm.

"You're a friend of Sam's?" he asks.

"Yes," I say, surprised that he knows. "I'm Jess." I want to ask how he knew.

"We're praying for your father," he says.

Thank you comes to my lips but not out of my mouth. Instead I say, "I don't know how to pray." I say it so low, I'm not sure I've spoken the words. Father Killen hears me somehow. Maybe priests have extra-strong hearing so they can listen to things people don't even voice.

He speaks to me, not seeming to worry about the people behind me, waiting. As if we are alone on the steps.

"Prayer is something you practice. Follow the form, and the substance will come."

He must see how puzzled I am, for he adds, "Just start, Jess. 'Our heavenly father, I am . . . ' Of course, he already knows you. If you don't think you hear back, do it again and again. Sometimes it's a long way from our heart to God's ear, but it isn't God who's far away, it's us, and sometimes lighting a candle is a form of prayer."

Around us, people jostle politely, trying to get closer.

I nod and let the crowd move me downstream, until I find a quiet eddy and break away.

Sam finds me near the stand of crape myrtles in the peace garden. The name is right. Even though we're close to the entrance to the church, here the air is quiet. Even the road noise sounds muffled.

"Did you tell Father Killen about my dad?"

"Of course," Sam says.

"My dad's not Catholic."

"It doesn't matter."

"Oh," I say. Because I don't know what to say. Because maybe Sam has added my name to the prayer list, and I suddenly feel open and raw, like I scraped my skin.

"Jessica," a voice says.

Commander Butler. I hadn't seen him inside. He's not in uniform here, but everyone would know he's an officer in the military. He stands tall and straight. Even his voice is imposing.

"Yes, sir," I say. I want to tell him, *It's just Jess.* No one who knows me calls me Jessica, because my real name is Jess. That's what the paperwork said.

He starts over. "I wanted to tell you in person how sorry I am your dad's been wounded. Warren's a tough guy. He'll be back on his feet and into that uniform. No question." He seems to believe what he says, the way Father Killen did.

"Thank you. We want to get back into the fundraising, too," I say.

Sam inhales sharply, and I realize I've said something I shouldn't have.

"We've all had a shock," Commander Butler says. "And we do have to rally around our military families." He pauses. "I know you've worked really hard for the orphanage, and I wasn't going to say anything here. But, since you mentioned it, I think under the circumstances . . ." His voice trails off. "Under the circumstances" is how adults condense all the bad things into three words that sound so plain. As if three words can contain everything that's happened since yesterday.

If I walk away, then he can't say the words I know are coming. But my body won't move.

"I have to ask you to take a hiatus from the charity drive. Folks around here don't want to be reminded of the orphanage at the moment. It's like an open wound."

"But it isn't the orphans' fault."

Commander Butler shifts his weight from one foot to the other. The same way Sam does when someone says something he disagrees with. That's where Sam must get it.

From the corner of my eye, I see Sam start to shift. He knows what's coming too.

"I have to take into account everyone on post. I've been specifically asked to consider the feelings of others about the orphanage, Jess. Not just the people involved in Operation Oleander."

"Who?" The woman who complained we were manipulating peoples' emotions? The man who brushed our poster from its stand as he hurried his pregnant wife away?

"It was Mr. Scott."

An invisible punch hits my stomach.

"But—" He supported the idea. Maybe he forgot how Mrs. Scott enjoyed stopping by the orphanage. "Corporal Scott cares"—I catch myself—"cared about the orphanage."

"No one doubts that. We all do. But for now I have to ask you to stand down."

"Stand down?" As if I am a soldier.

"Yes."

"But—"

"Jessica, I'm commander of the post. Everyone on Fort Spencer is my responsibility. First and foremost, the welfare of my troops and fulfillment of our mission.

Relations with indigenous populations — local inhabitants like those children at the orphanage — that's a role for civilian agencies. Not combat soldiers. The rules over there are changing."

"You think they did something wrong." I'm not asking a question. The words shoot out of my mouth. Images from the television report flicker across my vision. "My dad would never dishonor the military."

Sam's eyes are like the owl's again. Sad and knowing. He'd known his father felt this way, and he didn't warn me. Did he plan that we'd run into his dad?

"I know that. Warren's an honorable man. But there will be a review of interactions between soldiers and civilians. In hopes we can avoid something like this ever happening again."

"A review? How long will we have to stand down?"

Beside me Sam is fairly tap-dancing in place, he's so tense.

But Commander Butler isn't shifting anymore. His body is planted tall and rigid. "Until I give the all clear. If I do. Be patient. There may be other options. The review will be fair."

I stand still, my hands at my sides. If I were a soldier, I'd have to salute him back and say, "Yes, sir."

But I'm not.

"Tell your dad we're behind him," Commander Butler says.

"When he gets out of the coma."

If.

Sam breaks. "Jess," he says.

But his dad doesn't react. My words bounce off him like small pebbles pinging against armor.

"We'll give you a ride home," Commander Butler says. "Mrs. Butler's ordered an ice cream detour."

He means to offer me an olive branch.

I don't take it. "Mrs. Johnson's waiting for me over on the next block. I'd better go. Thank you." I make myself turn and walk away.

"See you later, Jessica," Commander Butler says.

I wince.

"Dad." I hear Sam's voice. "Jess. Her name's Jess. Did we have to talk about this today?"

I walk faster because I don't want to hear anything else Commander Butler has to say about me or the operation. I should be glad for Sam to even question his dad.

It doesn't help.

That night, after Cara goes to sleep, I wander into the living room because Mrs. Johnson's talking back to the television.

"Get a load of this," she says, waving at the local news channel like an angry hockey fan. "What a bunch of hooey."

"What?"

She edges up the volume. "Last week we reported on the deaths and injuries of U.S. soldiers in Kabul when a car bomb exploded outside an orphanage near the market," says the newscaster. "Now allegations have surfaced among Afghani witnesses. They say they not only saw soldiers tossing toys and pencils to children but that at least one of the soldiers threw something right before the larger bomb exploded. One witness alleges it was a grenade. During the Soviet invasion of Afghanistan, decades ago, bombs made to look like toys were responsible for the dismemberment and/or death of thousands of children. Other witnesses deny the soldiers did anything wrong and say they are victims in the same way the orphanage is."

"That's right. Those other 'witnesses' are lying." I find myself speaking to the reporter as if he can hear me. Just like Mrs. Johnson's doing.

Mrs. Johnson turns up the volume even more.

I plop onto the couch.

The news anchor continues. "Locals familiar with the

orphanage say that, if nothing else, the Americans are to blame for the orphanage becoming a target. At least five children and an Afghan teacher were killed, in addition to the U.S. casualties."

Five children. My head swirls as I try to conjure the faces of the children at the orphanage. No word yet on Warda. Sam said he would let me know. Does he mean it? But five children. That's the first word we've heard on casualties at the orphanage.

An Afghani man speaks on camera. "This is how America works. It's as bad as if they bombed the building themselves. We want to be paid fairly for the damage caused by the U.S."

Another man pipes up behind him. "The soldiers kill the children."

"We didn't bomb the orphanage," I say. "That doesn't even make any sense."

"Of course not, Jess," Mrs. Johnson says. "This is what I mean. It doesn't pay to meddle. To do something good. Foreigners don't appreciate it."

My eyes sting as though from smoke. It's horrible enough that the explosion killed Meriwether's mother and Private Davis and injured Dad. How can anyone blame the unit? They were trying to do something good. It doesn't make any sense.

The camera cuts back to the announcer at the news desk. She's wearing a pink blouse and lipstick the shade of cotton candy. She peers into the camera as if she's selling cosmetics, not hard-hitting news.

"We're waiting for information from the general on the ground. So far, 'no comment' is all we've been told. On background, we've been advised that they'll wait for an investigation to review what happened. But, off the record, U.S. officials categorically deny any wrongdoing. The investigation is intended to clear up what happened."

Investigation.

I shiver. That's what Commander Butler said. Will they want to talk to Dad when he regains consciousness? To me?

Crazy. The accusations are just crazy. Part of me wants to go straight back down to the PX and pull out the display again. Write in big letters on oversize poster board about the good that Operation Oleander has done. The milk goat, the school supplies. I'd tape it high on the front of the building, where everyone would see that Dad and the others had been doing good things for the children of Afghanistan. And they were attacked for doing it.

But I watch the scenes again on the screen. I think about foreign troops driving up in a Humvee toward the orphanage for girls. Down windy, dusty streets where people peer out from screenless windows, afraid. Where they watch from shadows to see what is happening. Who's there? Is it the Taliban? Someone to rob them or take their sons?

And a Humvee of soldiers carrying guns and what must look like military supplies in boxes sealed over so you can't see what's inside stops outside the orphanage. The soldiers get out.

Hidden faces watch them. They are the enemy. Their planes have bombed villages by accident. Killed people unintentionally. That is war.

I press my fingers against my eyes. When I open them again, tiny black dots soar across my vision.

My bones ache, I am so tired.

Maybe they're right. Maybe things are too confused right now to be able to tell whether we're doing something good or not. I don't know what to do.

"I'm going to bed," I say.

"Sounds good. I don't know why I tuned in to this, anyway. But I can't go to sleep now. I'm going to watch something light. Want to stay up?"

"No, thanks."

"Well, good night." Mrs. Johnson's voice sounds disappointed, as if she is lonely too.

I lie in bed with the door cracked open so I can see

into the hallway. Light from the television screen flashes against the darkness, a little the way fireworks do, casting light onto a night sky. When I close my eyes and try to talk to God the way Father Killen suggested, I can still see the white fragments in the dark hallway like shooting stars.

THIRTEEN

I DREAM OF fireworks. Explosions and candlelight flicker through my brain. I roll over and turn on my flashlight. Across the room, Cara's sprawled out across her toddler bed, as if she fell asleep doing jumping jacks in bed. The fingers of one of her hands curl around her toy dolphin.

Inching open the bottom drawer in my nightstand, I find all the photos I've taken with my camera since we moved to post. I huddle over them and scan them with my flashlight. Meriwether and me in oversize sunglasses in front of wiggly mirrors at the amusement park. Swimming off the coast, where she managed to get a photo of the two of us in facemasks and snorkels, grinning despite the gear. In Tarpon Springs, at the oceanography club, where Meriwether stuffed sponges inside her swim top.

The other photos include Sam and us at the post pool. Sam standing on his sailboat like a pirate. Finally, there's one of Meriwether and her parents sitting together under the fairy lights in the Scotts' backyard last summer after we finished installing them. Close-ups of day lilies. *Hemerocallis.* "Beauty for a day" in Greek.

Maybe if I put together an album for Meriwether, she'll remember the good times we had. If she and her dad really do move away, she might want to look at it sometimes. Maybe she'll remember we're friends.

With all the photos next to me in bed, sorted into two stacks, I close my eyes again and try to sleep.

"Rise and shine."

Morning. Mrs. Johnson is trying to imitate reveille. Not at all like Dad does it, with a real horn.

She knocks — at least she does that before she peers around the partially open bedroom door.

"We're going out. So rise and shine."

Cara wakes up and grins like a jack-in-the-box. Her hair is a mess — strands of it stick straight up right where the cowlick swirls at the crown of her head. She's still wearing the Cinderella pajamas. But she springs out of bed, ready to go.

"Where to?" I ask. I imagine the PX, and I'm not ready to go back there.

"Shopping."

"The PX?"

"No. Off post."

"What if my mom calls?" My voice is tight, taut as Sam's sailboat rope when the wind pushes the mainsail.

"She'll leave a message. If it's important, we can call back."

I feel the photos next to me. Overnight the two stacks slid together, and I'll have to sort them again. "Could we go to the craft store?"

Mrs. Johnson grins as if all her attempts to spark some interest have paid off. "Sure, maybe an organizer for those." She nods toward my photos.

"How about an album?"

"Sure, we can do that. Maybe you should send some to your dad."

I don't say anything to her about the photos. Not these. Because these are for Meriwether.

"We could get some finger paints for Cara too," Mrs. Johnson adds.

"Not finger paints," I say, throwing her a warning glance.

Cara's face closes up tight as a day lily bud, and her bottom lip puffs out.

"It'll be okay, Jess," Mrs. Johnson says. "That's what drop cloths are for."

Cara jumps up and down, laughing.

I close my eyes.

Three hours later we're back, and I dash into the house, my Crafty World package in my hand. I bought a photo album for Meriwether and some card stock and stickers, to make a get-well card for Dad.

"I'm going to work in my room," I call over my shoulder.

"Jess, where's the drop cloth?"

"On the utility shelves," I yell down the hall.

I'm unpacking the blue album, lifting the plastic cover off of it and inhaling the new, fresh scent of it, when I remember.

The utility shelves.

No. I don't want Mrs. Johnson out there. She might snoop around. She might look in the old cooler where my baby photos are stored.

Dashing out to the carport, I call after her. All I can see is her backside where she's leaning over a box. I can't see for sure, but I think it's the Christmas ornament box.

"It's up top. On the shelf." Near my dad's workbench.

Mrs. Johnson groans as she cranks herself upright. "Creaky old back. Thanks, Jess."

I wait until she lifts the drop cloth off and closes the utility-closet door behind her.

My face goes red, as if she might guess why I'm suddenly so helpful when I warned her against the finger paints to begin with. "Okay, I'm going to work on my album," I say.

I organize the photos, starting with last year's oceanography camp. Underneath each one I print where we were or who was with us, or what day it was. I try to remember every detail. The scent of half-dry bathing suits hanging from makeshift clotheslines across our cabin. They looked like a booby trap meant to snare rival cabin girls sneaking inside to play pranks. The grit of sand underneath bare feet. No matter how often we swept the tile floor with the frayed broom, the floor was always sandy and damp, as if the tide itself swept in and receded twice a day, leaving behind traces of the gulf.

One photo taken in front of the cabin was of all the girls in our group — we were the Dolphins. Other cabins were sea turtles and gulls and sand dollars. We came from all over Florida — Pensacola, Clementine, Miami, and Tallahassee. We promised to write, and even did a few times.

Most recently, one of the girls, Cece, had written to Meriwether and me to ask whether we were coming back this summer. She wanted to reserve the Dolphin cabin again and hoped we would be there.

The evening before the photo was taken, we'd gone for a night swim, supervised by the camp counselors. Meriwether protested that we didn't need babysitters.

The sea at night is different. The water felt warmer somehow, and if I closed my eyes and floated, I almost didn't think about what might be underneath me in the dark water. Moonlight flickered across the surface, and I imagined Meriwether and me following the moon's reflection to the edge of the sky. Together we watched the phosphorescence when the surf crested and fell onto the shore. The whole night seemed magical.

Afterward, we changed into sweatpants and stayed up late eating s'mores. The camp counselors gave us each a twine necklace with a dolphin charm as a memento. Then we wrote our dreams on pieces of paper and tossed them into the fire to send our dreams skyward. We didn't share our secrets about what we'd written. Not even Meriwether and me.

The phone rings, and I jump.

Mom.

I pull myself away from the camp and run for the phone in the living room.

"Hello?"

"Jess, I have a surprise for you." Mom's voice is light and fizzy as seltzer.

"Hello?" Mrs. Johnson's picked up in the kitchen.

"It's my mom. You can hang up," I say.

"Jess, it's okay," Mom says. "Libby, I hope the girls are being good."

I dare Mrs. Johnson to tell Mom everything.

"Oh, we're all doing fine. Just fine," she says.

She doesn't tell her all the little things.

"Mom, what about the surprise?"

"Hold on now," she says. I hear rustling on the other end of the line, like something burrowing through tall grass. "Here he is!"

"Dad?" Really, it's him?

Something crackles on the line.

"I'll hang up now." Mrs. Johnson clicks off.

Now it's just me.

And dead air.

"Dad?"

Mrs. Johnson stands in the doorway from the kitchen. I turn away so she can't see my face.

"Dad?" I hear my own voice rise in tone.

I hear something over the line. Something faint. Too low for me to make out words. Maybe he's talking and I just can't hear him.

"We can't wait for you to come home. I got the photos you sent." I fill the silence in case it's him.

"Je-ess." I think that's what he's saying. It comes out like "Jess" but also like "yes."

"It's me, Dad."

Had the bombing affected the way he talks? Maybe he doesn't remember the bombing. What if he doesn't know Meriwether's mother was killed?

"Dad?" Still silence.

"Jess." Mom's back on the line. "Your dad's resting again. But did you hear him, Jess? Didn't you hear him?" Her voice has a hoarseness in it, a voice that wants something to be true.

"I heard him." Maybe I really did.

Mrs. Johnson edges closer.

"When are you coming home, Mom?"

"Soon. I'm sure it'll be soon." She repeats the word "soon" as if it's a magic phrase and will come true.

"Mom —" I want to ask Dad about Operation Oleander. What I should do. About the investigation and what it means.

"Jess, I'm glad you didn't upset your dad. Now, I'd better talk to Mrs. Johnson. Get the real scoop on Cara. Is she there?"

"She's here. Bye, Mom." I pass the receiver to Mrs. Johnson.

I go back to my room and sign the card to Dad. Then I continue arranging all the photos in the album and writing notes under each one. I draw Meriwether's name in curlicues the way she writes her own name and Caden's when she thinks I'm not looking.

I finish and wrap the album in plastic in case it rains and head out the door.

This time, I hope she listens.

FOURTEEN

T HE DRAGONFLY lawn ornament that bobbed in the front garden at the Scotts' house is gone. Did Meriwether do that? Or was it her dad? Or some stranger who came to the door? Someone's also taken down most of the ribbons from the porch railing, but the wreath on the front door remains. So does the American flag, though it hangs limp in the humid air.

Suddenly, the world is still. Airless. Not a breath stirs.

I imagine it's this way only around Meriwether's house. Nowhere else.

I knock, feel the weight of the photo album in the bag on my shoulder.

The curtains don't move on the inside of the windows.

I wait and knock again.

Come on, Meriwether. Please open the door.

Without warning, the door flies away from me.

Mr. Scott stands there, one hand still on the door-knob. Cool air from inside flows toward me like water.

"Mr. — Mr. — Scott."

"Jess," he says. "I didn't expect you."

Does that mean he doesn't want me here?

"I'm sorry." Those are the only words that will come out of my mouth.

"I am too," he says. His face has no muscles, his eyes no expression. "And about your dad. I hope he pulls through."

I nod. We both nod.

"Is Meriwether home?" The afternoon heat presses down on me, even though the clouds are building over-head, silent and towering.

He looks away. "Meriwether's not here right now."

"Oh."

We stand on opposite sides of the door. Neither of us moves.

"Is she coming back soon?" Maybe she went to the pool. Or the beach. Maybe I can find her there.

Mr. Scott rubs his face, hard. "Jess," he starts. He stops.

I wait, my skin absorbing the heat from the sun the way it does when I sit in a hot car for too long. Melting hot. The colors in the photos might run if it stays this hot.

"I don't . . ." His voice fades.

"I can come back," I say. "Maybe tonight." She'll be home then.

He shakes his head. "Maybe you — "

Something inside the house howls in frustration like a caged animal. "Forget it, Dad."

Meriwether.

Her voice calls from deep inside. From her room. "Tell her to come in."

She's home after all.

The album burns a hole in my tote bag.

Mr. Scott opens the door wider and shrinks back to let me pass. I have to walk through.

My legs don't want to move. Coming here was a mistake.

One foot and then the other through the door. The cool air envelops me. I am radioactive — that's what Meriwether is thinking.

At the doorway to Meriwether's room I pause. Suddenly, it seems stupid, this gift I've brought.

The throw pillows have been tossed everywhere, as if someone was looking for a valued object hidden in the room. Meriwether has her back to me. On her bed, a roll-on bag lies unzipped. The comforter underneath it half drags onto the floor. The blue medallion sheets have pulled away from the corners. No one could bounce a quarter off the sheets the way army recruits are supposed to.

"Why did you come over?" Meriwether asks.

"You're my friend."

Meriwether's laugh is strangled.

"You're coming back, right?" I have to ask.

"We're leaving in a couple of hours for Dover. I told you that. Dad wants to get there before the plane does." The plane with her mother's body in it.

I remember footage of a jet arriving at Dover months ago with bodies of fallen soldiers inside. An honor guard meets every plane and escorts each casket from the plane to inside the waiting area, then to a hearse, then to a commercial flight that takes the fallen soldier home.

In my head I see the tarmac when the plane arrives with Meriwether's mother and Private Davis. The sun will have gone down, but the asphalt will still feel summer-soft underfoot. I imagine I am with the Scotts, waiting for the slow march of soldiers' boots to the aircraft. The steps in unison. The quiet respect, eternal silences between each step. Wondering what I would do if it were my dad.

"Jess, I don't want to go." Meriwether's voice suddenly sounds frightened, like a little kid's.

"It's important." *Duty, honor, country.*

Love.

Meriwether folds a dress into the suitcase. "You don't know what I did," she says.

"What do you mean?"

"Remember those stupid letters Ms. Rivera made us write?"

"Yes." I do remember. I slipped my dad's into his duffel bag. The day they deployed. Meriwether did the same thing. We agreed.

"I lied to you. I didn't put it in Mom's bag."

"Okay." I frown. "It's not a big deal."

"It is." Meriwether clutches a pair of jeans in her hands and looks at me. "She was trying to do all these things for me. A dress for eighth-grade graduation, months away. How crazy was that? All the clothes at the stores were fall and winter. Then we went bathing suit shopping with you. She was trying to make up in advance for missing things, and I got so mad about that."

"That's okay." At home, Mom had been short with Dad too a few days before he left. It had left me dizzy with fear. I ran down the block to get away from their argument. When I walked back home, it was over, and we ate pizza like nothing had happened.

"It isn't okay," Meriwether says, her voice rising. "I

told her I didn't care. I hated her making me do all those things. I didn't want her to go."

"But you did care." Mrs. Scott knew that. She'd look at me when Meriwether was yanking clothes off the rack and smile. Because even an irritated Meriwether was worth being with.

"I didn't tell her."

"She knew."

"I didn't tell her, and I can't ever tell her." Meriwether's words strike me like fastballs. One after the other.

I step into the room.

"Meriwether." I reach for her arm, and the shoulder bag, the album inside, tugs against my body.

"She called me the other day. Before." Meriwether's voice dips suddenly quiet. All the heat is gone. The words she says sit cold like air conditioning.

Dad called us last week too. The reception that day was bad. His voice sounded tinny. But we'd watched him talk over the Internet connection. He was happy to tell us about the orphanage.

"I hung up on her," Meriwether says. "I was so mad she'd reenlisted. She didn't have to. She didn't have to go."

I am standing on the brink of a high ledge. I don't know how far down I will fall if I step forward over the abyss. From far below, the sound of rushing water reaches my ears.

"She called back. She left a message on the machine because I wouldn't pick up. If I hadn't been a brat, I would have picked up the phone and talked to her."

I remember the sound of Mrs. Scott's voice on the answering machine.

"But she left you a message," I say. If it was for me, I'd play it over and over. I'd make copies and put them in different places so I could listen to them. So I'd never lose them.

The expression on Meriwether's face is hollow. "I erased it without listening to it."

No.

"I can't unerase the message," she says. "I can't take it back, Jess. I can't ever listen to it again."

Meriwether teeters, and I throw my arms around her body.

What if we hadn't done what we did? What if we hadn't started Operation Oleander? What if? What if? The voices in my head won't stop. Is Meriwether saying the words or am I?

Together, we fall over the edge toward the rushing emptiness beneath us, and I won't let go.

FIFTEEN

INSIDE THE cemetery, cars park along the winding drive, which is lined with flags. I follow people walking toward a canopied seating area. Folding chairs are planted in rows like the white grave markers all around us. If I squint, it looks like an optical illusion — white squares fanning out all the way to the far end of the fence. The heat shimmers across the grass.

The crowd moves around me like a river, and I am caught up in the flow of it. Until we make it to the canopy. There I stand on tiptoe in the back, trying to find Sam, to see Meriwether. Meanwhile, the casket has been carried in and placed on a stand. A large U.S. flag lies draped across the top, just like the footage from television showed when the military plane landed at Dover.

Then I see her. Meriwether. And her dad. They're

sitting in the first row, just in front of the casket. An elderly couple sits beside them, their bodies bent from it all. From the word from Afghanistan. From waiting for the body to be flown to Dover and then again to here. From the way everything has moved around them in slow motion.

Meriwether's wearing her navy blue graduation dress, the one her mother picked out when we went shopping.

The air smells of summer grass, just mown. The groundskeepers must have cut it this morning when the grass was still wet with dew. Salt hangs in the air too, off the gulf. Now and then the breeze picks up the scent of thick, sweet lilies spilling from flower arrangements.

There should be day lilies.

A movement to the left catches my eye. Commander and Mrs. Butler have arrived, Sam behind them wearing a white shirt and a black tie. Walking stiffly, he and his parents walk to the front row, and the commander speaks to Mr. Scott and to Meriwether, and her grandparents. Then they take their seats across the aisle from them.

I'm supposed to go there and sit with Sam. But my legs won't move. If I sit there, I will witness everything up close. Grief will press against me from all sides like the humidity.

Sam sits straight in the chair, but he sees me. He doesn't wave, but he nods his head when I catch his glance. He motions me his way.

I point to the spot where I'm standing.

What did the commander just say to Meriwether and her dad, anyway? Had Mrs. Scott wanted to go to the orphanage that morning? Or did she just go along with my dad, restless while waiting to convoy out? Or had my dad asked her?

Had Dad asked because I sent that last box of pencils?

A minister calls for the opening prayer.

Commander Butler speaks next. "Today we honor a brave soldier who epitomized duty and sacrifice. She never shirked that duty, and she found time and a passion for serving others. Not just as a soldier but as a daughter, a wife, and a mother." He pauses, and when I open my eyes, he is looking down at his paper.

"Corporal Scott also wanted to help others. On the day she was killed, she was going to be carrying out a special mission, along with others from Fort Spencer. But that morning was a mission of mercy, of compassion. She didn't stop to ask what was in it for her. She didn't do it for duty or honor or even for country. She and Private Davis and Master Sergeant Westmark — they each one traveled those dangerous streets of Kabul that morning for a reason larger than the United States Army they served. They undertook that risk to serve others less fortunate than we are. For those who are the most innocent among us, children caught in a war they do not understand and from which they cannot protect themselves. They did it for reasons we don't often talk about in uniform. They did it for love."

The heavy air trapped under the tent presses against my skin. The commander talks about the orphanage, about my dad and Mrs. Scott. I didn't think he'd mention my dad, or that he would describe what happened with the words he used. "Sacrifice" and "compassion" and "love." I see the marketplace in my head and try to find hope and promise in those burned-out images, in the smoke from the Humvee.

"On that day," the commander says, "the forces that signify the worst of human nature came to the fore and snuffed out the lives of Corporal Scott and Private Davis. But those forces cannot destroy the life force behind what led Corporal Scott to the orphanage that day. So today we honor her and her commitment, a commitment that we must also honor by preserving her memory, by carrying on her mission. And by living that life of example for her daughter — Meriwether — so she will remember her mother through her actions. Who she was. What she stood for."

The commander's words echo in my ears. *Commitment. Carrying on her mission. What she stood for.* Doesn't that also mean Operation Oleander, not only her role as a soldier? Does the commander mean those words for me?

In the silent spaces between Commander Butler's words, I hear a sob. Not from Meriwether but from her grandmother.

Then I hear something else. A rustling. A murmur. Coming from behind us.

A girl has moved to stand next to me. It's the blond girl from the PX, the one who tried to help me. She tugs on my arm.

"You have to look," she says. "Now."

I turn. A group of people are marching toward the canopy. At first I think they are mourners, late arrivals.

But they're carrying signs and banners.

"Who are they?" the girl whispers.

Others in the back rows crane their necks to see what's happening. People seated in front of them, unaware of what's coming, turn and shush them.

The commander continues, but I can't hear him anymore.

Protesters.

A man says, "I can't believe they're here. Come on." He motions to some of the soldiers standing in the back row. They fan out in a line, close together, not talking.

The oncoming group splinters as if to flank our position. Men and women, even little kids, carry signs.

A little blond boy's sign reads GOD HATES YOU! Another one says THANK GOD FOR DEAD SOLDIERS. A woman waves a placard: GOD IS GLAD CORPORAL SCOTT IS DEAD. SHE DIED BECAUSE OF YOUR SINS. YOU ARE ALL GOING TO HELL.

I breathe in, but the air around the canopy has become something solid.

The soldiers lock hands, creating a perimeter to keep the demonstrators back from the graveside. They don't move to meet the marchers, but they're waiting. A silent, steady line.

"Where are the police?" I ask the woman in front of me. "Can't they do something?"

"They won't interfere," she says. "Unless there's violence. It's a public place. Those Angustus Church members are crazy. A cult. They have no decency. But they get their First Amendment rights to protest the war."

People can disagree about the war, I know that. I've seen protestors wave flags and march down the street. But demonstrators can call out about God being glad Corporal Scott is dead? At her *funeral?* Who are these people? How can they believe what they're saying?

Others under the canopy begin to realize what's happening. What if these people had come and it was my dad's funeral?

"I'm afraid," the girl says. "What if they attack?"

"You know Sam, right?" I ask the girl.

"Yes."

"Go stand next to him. Nothing can bother you there. His dad's the commander," I say.

The girl touches my arm. "You come too?"

"In a minute," I say. But as soon as I say the words, I know I'm lying.

Because I'm not going in that direction.

The minister has started a final prayer. His baritone voice is deep and carries over the hum. He's projecting louder than before, as if he knows he has to compete, not with jets overhead but with the Angustans.

Everyone seated stands.

I nudge the girl forward. "Go on."

She nods and slips through the lines of mourners in front of us. She moves like a piece of music on the air.

I step out from under the canopy, into the glare. Facing the oncoming marchers, who look like soldiers, my knees shake, but I won't retreat.

Instead, I run toward and then under the interlocked arms of the soldiers who are between the gravesite and the protesters. I raise my arm as if I am carrying a battle flag of my own into hand-to-hand combat.

But I have nothing to wave back and forth in the air that's stronger than their signs. Nothing that's stronger than their anger.

 SIXTEEN

T HE PROTESTER closest to me is a blond teenage boy.

"You're not too young to burn in hell," he says. "You're a sinner." He thrusts his sign into the air and waves it back and forth, taunting me. The picture on the front is a grainy photo of Corporal Scott, the way it would look if someone had cut her photo out of the newspaper and enlarged it. In the photo, she's wearing her uniform. Her hair is smooth and close cut, and she's smiling. But her teeth are blotted out, as if the boy has covered over them with a black marker.

I blink in the light. Anger oozes out of my skin like sweat. How can they do this?

TODAY, SATAN GETS A NEW SOUL the poster reads in uneven letters. It's written in childlike print, where the letters don't all fit right but squish together at the end.

I jump and reach for the poster. When I grab a corner, it rips in my hand. Just a piece of it.

The boy steps back, laughing. He holds the sign up higher. Even though it's torn, he displays it like a badge of honor.

Around me protesters are calling out Corporal Scott's name as a sinner. Mr. Scott must hear them. And Meriwether. I want to protect her the way I would Cara. Or Warda.

The protesters have to be stopped.

I jump into the air again, stretch toward the poster. Toward the black glare of anger.

"Jess!"

I hear my name, but the short blond hair of the boy in front of me is all I see. I smell his breath in the air. It's sweet — not what I expected. It should be sour and putrid, the way evil is supposed to smell.

I reach for the poster, but it slips between my fingers this time without tearing. I stumble, empty-handed, trying to catch my balance.

"That's right," the boy says. "You can't overcome the power of God."

"You don't represent the power of God." I'm sure Father Killen would agree.

"God judges the good and the evil. Today he has judged Corporal Scott and Private Davis and condemned them." The words tumble out of his mouth like Scripture he has memorized the words to, but not the meaning.

I stretch out my hands, not for the poster this time.

I reach for the boy.

That's when someone grabs my arms and pulls me back before I can make contact.

The boy laughs.

"Jess, it's what they want." It's Sam's voice in my ear. Somehow he found me.

I twist out of his grasp. He pulls my arm, and we're moving upstream, back toward the canopy.

"How can they do this? To Meriwether—to all of us?"

"I don't know, Jess. But we don't want to make it worse."

"How could it be worse?"

"The press," Sam says. He points to a van that's parked on the perimeter road. A satellite dish sprouts out of the top like a strange vegetable.

"Good. Let the reporters tell the world about these horrible people."

"They'll tell the world you attacked them," Sam says.

I wrench free of Sam's grasp, but I continue walking

back toward the funeral. I hate that he's right. I shield my face from someone holding a camera. Turn away from a woman with a microphone.

My head hurts. What if Dad sees me on television from Germany? Will he think I did the right thing? Do I?

The minister has finished.

Behind us, the soldiers still stand shoulder to shoulder. The cult members jeer at them, but they don't react. Just like the wall of protection they've created, like a breakwater.

"Why don't they make the protesters stop?" I ask Sam.

"Discipline," Sam says, as if that's a good thing.

"You would say that." Was it just that Sam was a commander's son? Or was it more than that? Maybe Sam's just a rules-and-order person. His world is black and white. "I'm glad I'm not in the army."

"I bet the army is too." Then Sam smiles at me, just a little, and he nudges my shoulder.

The honor guard marches forward in unison. Their rifles snap to their shoulders as if they're one.

The three-volley salute is fired. I cover my ears after the first shot. Next to me, Sam stares straight ahead, his arms at his sides. On his other side, the girl from the PX jumps at each shot.

In front of us, Mr. Scott and Meriwether sit tall and straight. They stare ahead. Meriwether doesn't even flinch.

Afterward, the bugler plays taps while a soldier folds the American flag and hands it to Mr. Scott.

> *Fades the light; and afar*
> *Goeth day, and the stars*
> *Shineth bright,*
> *Fare thee well; day has gone,*
> *Night is on.*

The words come to me, though I don't want them to.

"Come on," Sam says. "Let's get in line." Mourners are filing by the Scotts to pay their respects.

My feet go in the right direction. I'm walking in a bad dream and I can't stop.

"It's my fault, isn't it?" I say the words out loud. The words that have circled around me like a swarm of mosquitoes, droning in my ear. Day after day, gathering strength.

We step closer to the front of the line.

"It's not your fault, Jess. You didn't detour to the orphanage that day."

"So it's my dad's fault?" My voice rises.

"I didn't say that," Sam says, his voice softer as if to counterbalance mine. "Come on, we're almost there."

In front of us, the girl from the PX has made it to the family. She shakes the grandparents' hands. She speaks to Meriwether, who stands there, back stiff. She's holding the folded flag.

I can't tell what she's saying to Meriwether. But she's listening, because she nods once or twice. Other mourners weave around the two of them. The girl finishes, and when she looks my way, her eyes are shiny as wet grass.

"What's her name?" I nudge Sam's arm. Sam knows all the kids on post practically, since his dad's the commander. Sam and Mrs. Butler often meet the whole family, not just the service member.

"Aria. Her dad just left for Afghanistan."

"Oh." What did Aria say to Meriwether that made her listen?

In the last video Dad sent, even Warda had smiled for the first time I'd seen. A timid smile, as if she didn't trust herself to move her mouth upward. Then the bombing happened. If Warda is still alive, will she trust enough to smile again? Does she hate American soldiers? Or blame me?

Suddenly, it's our turn. I follow Sam's lead, holding myself back.

First we pass by the grandparents. When Sam steps on, I reach out my hand to them, but words don't come out of my mouth.

They whisper "Thank you for coming," a line they must have been repeating all day. Meriwether's grandfather wears dark sunglasses. Her grandmother has black smudges under her eyes. When our hands meet, she touches my arm with both of hers. Whether for her support or for mine I can't tell.

The blond boy with the protest sign looms in my mind. How could he do what he did? Doesn't he think of his own mother or father when he carries those posters of dead soldiers to their funerals?

But are we so different?

I am Sergeant Westmark's daughter. The one to blame for your daughter being at the wrong place at the wrong time. Me. Maybe I am the face of evil too.

If Meriwether's grandmother wonders about me, who I am, she doesn't ask.

"Thank you again for coming," she repeats in a voice fragile as moth's wings.

And, then, before I am ready, Sam steps toward Mr. Scott, and I stand before Meriwether.

She clutches the flag that draped her mother's coffin close to her heart. With her right hand she reaches out to shake mine. As if she doesn't recognize me.

I take her hand. Even in the heat, her hands are cold.

"Meriwether, it's me, Jess."

When I say her name, her eyelids flicker. I don't release her hand. I lean in close to her.

"She knows, Meriwether. Your mom knows you love
her." Present tense. I say the words.

Meriwether nods, but her eyes don't meet mine. Behind me, others are waiting for the line to move ahead. I
let her hand go, finally, and step down the line.

Mr. Scott shakes my hand too. Formal, as if I am not
the girl who spent long summer evenings in their backyard under the magic white lights before Mrs. Scott deployed. I whisper "I'm sorry" and follow Sam out from
under the canopy.

SEVENTEEN

THAT NIGHT after supper the phone rings. I stand by the door to my bedroom, listening for Mrs. Johnson to pick up. It's after midnight in Germany. If it's Mom, the news won't be good.

Maybe it's Meriwether.

My body presses into the door frame. After the funeral, I came home and went to my room. For once, Mrs. Johnson didn't lecture me. Or quiz me sixteen ways to Sunday about what happened at the funeral. At supper we ate without talking much either. Only Cara chattered the way she always does.

"Jess? It's Sam," Mrs. Johnson calls from the living room.

I take the call in the kitchen. Sam and I didn't say much on the way back from the funeral. Even Commander

Butler was quiet. They just dropped me off out front and headed home.

"Turn on the news," he says.

"Why?" Was there another bombing? More soldiers dead?

"They're running a piece on the protest."

"I'll call you back." I hang up and run into the living room. "Sam says there's something on the funeral."

Mrs. Johnson flips the channel to the local news, and there it is. Shots of the plane coming in, the long line of dark cars at the cemetery, and, finally, the Angustan protesters.

"I can't believe they showed up here, of all places," Mrs. Johnson says. "You didn't say much about them."

"Maybe we should turn it off," I finally say as the footage gets closer and closer to the protesters. The angle of the shot shows the blond kid. And then a shadow blurs past and a figure is running toward him. The camera catches the back of the person. It's a girl in a skirt. A girl with a ponytail. Her arm raises like a sword and slashes at the sign.

Mrs. Johnson sits there, not speaking, but her mouth drops open. This is the first time I've ever seen her with nothing to say. That should be funny. But not today.

I watch myself as if I'm someone else on the television footage.

"J — Jess?"

"I know. I couldn't help it. They made me so mad. Did you hear what they said? At a funeral?" The words fire like scattershot out of my mouth.

"I told you going was a mistake." Mrs. Johnson shakes her head. She sighs long and hard. *My fault.* She's thinking it was my fault. How is she going to explain this to my mother?

"Didn't you see those signs?" I say.

"Oh, I saw them."

We watch the replay, the shot where Sam grabs me. This time I see what happened after I turned away. The blond boy cheered. His face lit up like fireworks, white and bright, a starburst of celebration.

"Did you hit him?" Mrs. Johnson asks, her face flat as pancakes.

"No. But I wanted to."

She turns back to the television.

"I did rip his sign. A little." I wince, as if my hand is seared where I touched the poster.

Duty, honor, country. Where did my actions fall?

"Well, I think they deserved anything they got. But I don't want to burden your mother with this news. Heaven knows it'll be on Armed Forces Radio."

Fear scratches at my insides. Mom might see me on television in Germany.

And Dad.

Then he would know. Corporal Scott is dead. Private Davis, too.

The phone rings again.

I pick up. "Sam, I can't believe — "

"Hello?" The voice isn't Sam's. It's a woman's, clipped and proper. "Is this the Westmark residence?"

"Yes, this is the Westmark residence." My voice goes formal.

Mrs. Johnson cocks her head at an angle.

I shrug.

"This is Carmina Sanchez-Ryan. I'm with the *Clementine Times*, and I'd like to speak with Jessica Westmark."

"Jess Westmark. It's just Jess. That's me."

"Okay, just Jess. I'll make a note of that."

From her voice I can't tell if she's teasing me or not.

"As I was saying, I'm Carmina Sanchez-Ryan, and I want to do an article on Operation Oleander. A feature story."

The moisture in my mouth evaporates. *A feature story.*

The woman continues. "The piece would go in the People and Places section of our paper. You know, this is a local story with international connections."

When the woman pauses again, the silence stretches on and on.

"Yes." I say to say something. Anything.

"Oh, good. You're there. Thought I'd lost the connection. I always hit a dead zone along the parkway. Anyway, as I was saying, I understand you and your friends formed this group to help an orphanage in Kabul."

"We did." I know what comes next.

The bombing.

"I'd like to learn more about the operation."

What is there to say? It all ends the same way. Meriwether's mother and Private Davis dead. Dad injured. Who knows about the orphans. That part hasn't made the news yet.

A thought, a prayer, comes to me. Maybe if I talk to her, she could find out about the orphanage. Maybe some good could come out of publicity too. Something to counteract the Angustan group. Something to continue Operation Oleander's work.

"Tell me how you got started," she says.

"Well." I twist the cord in my hand. "Could you hold on just a minute?"

My hand over the receiver, I tell Mrs. Johnson about the reporter. "She wants to hear about Operation Oleander."

"My goodness. First the funeral and then the Angustans and you on television. Now a reporter's calling. What next, a plague of locusts?" Mrs. Johnson shakes her head. "What would your mother say?"

She harrumphs. Not a yes, but not a no, either. It's as if she has plausible deniability this way, the way they say it on the news. In case it turns out badly. She wriggles out of Dad's recliner, where she shouldn't be anyway, and heads outside. "For a smoke," she says over her shoulder.

"Okay," I say to the reporter. "I'm ready."

I plunge in and recount Dad's e-mails and photos of the orphanage they'd been near. I talk about Warda, too, and how I kept talking to Meriwether and Sam, getting them interested in wanting to help. First it was the goat, and then school supplies.

"Sam Butler? Commander Butler's son?" Her voice tweaks up at the end like a mongoose with a snake.

"Yes." I twist the cord harder. Suddenly, the story links Commander Butler to this charity group, and maybe he won't — certainly he won't — want to be part of it.

"And you said someone named Meriwether? Is that Meriwether Scott?"

I panic.

"Meriwether's going out of town. I don't think we should use her name in this."

"Okay, well, that's fine," she says, but her voice doesn't sound okay.

Guilt like a hot pepper slides down my insides, and I don't know what to do.

"It's just the three of you?"

"Um, yes." But not really, not anymore. Meriwether, she won't. And Sam, he was never that crazy about it.

"Do you have a photo of the orphanage?" she asks.

"Yes." Tons of photos. The one of Dad and Corporal Scott and Warda sears through my brain, like the blink of a camera flash. Another one shows the building — before the bomb — and the goat clambering over stones to reach some weeds. "I have some."

"Good. We'll see if we can use them. Now another question."

I hold my breath.

"The bombing."

Eyes closed. Focus on breathing. "Yes?"

"That was a tragedy. Followed by accusations of complicity by the United States. Maybe even that the U.S. caused the bombing. That's not supported by the facts, as far as I can tell, but sometimes facts don't matter." The woman laughs. "Well, don't quote me on that. Facts are my business. What now for Operation Oleander?"

With my free hand, I tug at the hem of my T-shirt, the way Cara does sometimes. What now? That's the question, isn't it?

"After what's happened, we're not sure." Weak answer.

"Unintended consequences. Yep, got that. If people want to help, and our readers here in Clementine are the best, what should they do?"

Do?

"Send money?" she asks.

"No, not money." After the goat, we focused on collecting in-kind items for school supplies. The military let us ship the boxes when space was available, and Dad took care of the rest. Now, after the bombing, there's no one to take the supplies, and everything is off-limits. And the investigation. Who knows where that will lead.

"Grass roots — I understand. Okay, how about we just refer people to the big international-relief efforts?"

"Okay."

"One last question. I heard talk of an investigation."

"Investigations are routine when tragedies happen and someone is killed," I say. "Soldier" doesn't come off my tongue.

"Do you think that will affect Operation Oleander?"

Of course it will. "We'll have to see," I say. My dad lies in the hospital in Germany, and Commander Butler said an investigation will look into what he and the others did with the orphanage and whether they drew the enemy there. Determine if they are to blame.

"Okay, well, you send that photo to me, one with the orphans," she says, and gives me her e-mail address.

"Will you send me the article? Before you print it?"

"That's not our policy," she says, suddenly all formal again.

"Can you find out about Warda?"

"The girl from the orphanage?"

"Yes." Had the Taliban killed her parents? Had they abandoned her at the orphanage? Did she know her own story? I knew mine, some of it. The official paperwork said my birth mother was too young, on her own, couldn't offer me a life. But I wondered about Warda.

"No promises. If the military hasn't said . . ." Her voice fades away. She means that if the military doesn't know or isn't saying, I'd better not get my hopes up.

"This is quite a story," she says.

"Please — please tell your readers what we were trying to do." It sounds lame. Good intentions, Mrs. Johnson would say. The road to you-know-where is paved with them.

"Well, I have to run, Jessica — I mean Jess."

She gets Jess right. But the proof of whether she gets

anything else right will be in the story. Maybe I shouldn't send the photograph. What if Warda's still alive and her photo gets splashed on the Internet for the Taliban to see? I flip through the photos looking for one that won't give the orphanage — or Warda — away.

EIGHTEEN

M OM FINALLY calls again the next morning. I get on the phone in the living room. Mrs. Johnson is talking to her on the kitchen phone.

"Hi," I say.

"Honey, I'm still talking to Mrs. Johnson. Like I said, Libby, I'm sorry it's been a few days. I've been waiting until I had some news to share."

News to share.

"We waited all yesterday for a consultation," she says.

"What's that mean?" I ask.

"A group meeting with all the doctors on your dad's case. The good news: They have a treatment plan. The better news? We're coming home in two weeks."

Two weeks. Just two more weeks.

I push down the voice in my head that asks me, "Then what?" and, "Will Dad still be able to work?" For now, I am so happy just that he is coming home.

"Can I talk to him?" Maybe this time he will talk back to me.

"He's sleeping right now. Why don't you send him an e-mail? We can read it when he wakes up."

We? Does that mean he can't see?

"What's the plan?" Mrs. Johnson asks.

"First he'll be transferred to the hospital there in Clementine."

"Another hospital?" I sink to the floor and wrap an arm around my knees. Mom had started with the good news. But there was the other foot, Mrs. Johnson would say.

"Just at first. They have to make sure your dad's stabilized. Then he can come home."

"After that?" I ask.

"We'll work it out." Mom's voice sounds like a cheerleader's. One more rah-rah for the team that's losing in the last quarter of the game.

"Mom, tell me."

The other end of the line is quiet.

Mrs. Johnson says from the other phone, "It's okay. Jess can handle it. Whatever it is. We all can."

My eyes blur. After everything, she's sticking up for me, and she's been there for my mom, too. That's what military families do. Her husband is still in Afghanistan.

"Your dad's lost his left eye." Her words hang in the air. "They had to remove it. They've done a lot of delicate surgery to keep the shrapnel from going into his brain. His other eye is damaged."

"Will Dad live?"

"Yes." Mom's voice sounds certain on that.

"Will he be blind?" I close my eyes, imagine not being able to see. What would happen to us then?

Mom is silent too long. Then she says, "We don't know yet how extensive the sight loss will be."

"Will Dad have to leave the army?"

The voice stops again. "He's afraid so. And that makes him sad, Jess. He hasn't really wanted to talk much since the last surgery. Your e-mails would help. I know it."

"Don't let Warren borrow trouble," Mrs. Johnson says. "There are lots of examples of injured soldiers being able to stay in the military. The army put all this money into Warren — they aren't going to toss him out because of one eye. Trust me." She says it with the force of a TV ad.

What would Dad do if he had to leave the army? What would we do?

"Jess, send your dad a note."

"I will."

As soon as we hang up, Mrs. Johnson puts her foot down, as she calls it.

"I want you out of the house. Today. Now. Go to the pool or the beach. Call Sam. I'll keep an eye on Cara." She glowers at me, but I see the gold flecks in her green eyes, and they aren't really angry. This is her mock-angry voice. The one that keeps trying to do the right thing.

"I need to write my dad an e-mail."

"Yes, you do. But not this moment. When you get back."

I surrender. "Okay."

She folds her arm, the glint in her eye like a tiny laser. "And where will you be going?"

First she wants me gone. Then she demands to know where.

"The beach. I want to go to the beach." And suddenly, I do want to go.

"Good. That's settled." Mrs. Johnson picks up the telephone handset. "Call Sam. Invite him."

Before the bombing, she wouldn't have wanted me to bother the commander's son, because we're just enlisted. As if we ourselves — Mrs. Johnson and I — are in the military too.

I dial, and Sam answers. "Want to go to the beach?"

"Sure. We can take the boat out too, just on the bay, though." Sam isn't allowed to take the boat out on the gulf. Not yet.

"To the island again?" The last time we were there was just a few weeks ago. Before the bombing. When Meriwether was still my friend.

Mrs. Johnson puts her hands on her hips. The good-cop act might not last. Not when she hears "island."

"I'll be there in twenty minutes," I tell Sam.

I'm readying my speech about why it's okay when Mrs. Johnson opens the refrigerator and pokes around inside. "Best I can offer is tuna salad on wheat. I can whip it up while you change into your swimsuit."

A picnic. It seems wrong.

But right now I want to go to the beach and sail with Sam to Cat Island. I want to tell him Dad is coming home. I want summer back to normal. And Mrs. Johnson is presenting it to me like a peace offering.

"Thanks." And I dash off to change clothes.

Sam's waiting for me when I get to the small marina near his house.

"I brought sandwiches!" I call to Sam over the sound of the wind whipping the water.

He holds up a red cooler and grins. "Sodas and freeze

tarts." A Mrs. Butler summer special of frozen limeade and sweet yogurt.

I turn back to the pier where the marina begins. Just for a second. As if I'm waiting for someone.

Meriwether. Normally, she'd be right here, going with us, the Three Musketeers. She'd be tiptoeing across the wooden planks to avoid getting her tiny heels stuck in between the cracks. Wearing fancy shoes because maybe she'd see Caden here.

Don't think that now. Maybe Meriwether will want to do something this week. Maybe all three of us can do something together.

Sam holds out his hand, steadies me as I step into the boat. It rocks gently under my weight.

As Sam's untying the boat from the dock a voice says, "Hey, Sam."

I shield my eyes from the sun. Caden. Of all days, and Meriwether isn't here.

Sam says hi, and I nod too.

"Have you seen Meriwether around?" he asks.

"Not since the funeral," Sam says.

Caden nods. "I didn't go. I — uh — is she out of town?"

Sam looks to me.

"I — I don't know." None of us talks about what happened.

"Okay, well, I just saw you over here. Know how you guys hang out together. Tell her I said hello."

"Sure," I say, keeping my voice plain and neutral, bland as vanilla yogurt. Before, Meriwether would have been thrilled to receive a message from Caden. Is the new Meriwether going to be as happy? I don't know.

After Caden leaves, Sam works the sails like a pro.

Half an hour later, we slide the boat onto shore at Cat Island. We find some shade beside the old fortress. Climbing on it is forbidden — safety reasons. Last year, Meriwether made us dig for treasure here, as if we were Cara's age. Sam and I groaned, but Meriwether was so excited, we couldn't help but enjoy it too. We dug holes around every foot of wall. It looked like giant crabs had invaded, there was so much sand piled high around each hole.

But no buried treasure.

"A reporter called me," I say.

Sam speaks around his bite of tuna sandwich. "What'd he want?"

"She. She wanted to ask me about Operation Oleander."

Sam swallows. "What did you tell her?"

"How we got started. About the goat, the school supplies."

"Did she say anything about my dad?" His voice is as hard as the coquina rock at our backs.

"She asked if your dad is Commander Butler. That's all. I didn't talk about your dad." Didn't *want* to talk about his dad. Sam looks at me like maybe I poisoned the tuna salad. "She asked me what we're going to do now."

Sam's gaze turns toward the post across the bay. "What did you tell her?"

"That I didn't know. There's no way to get supplies to the orphanage the way we did."

He dips his head slightly.

"She asked about the investigation, too."

This time Sam looks at me.

"You don't really think my dad's going to be in trouble, do you?" I ask.

"I don't know." He says it too fast.

"You do think so."

The air turns a shade cooler. A cloud has passed in front of the sun. Sam sees it too.

"We'd better get back." Unspoken is the truth that we don't want to be in a sailboat in a thunderstorm.

I jump up, but I grab his arm. "You think he's in trouble." My dad's enlisted. His is an officer. Not only that — he's the commander.

"No, I don't. Not after everything's that happened."

"You mean because he got hurt?"

"That's not what I mean," Sam says. He snatches up the cooler and heads for the boat.

I follow him, unable to say anything else about the future of what might happen with Dad.

That night, after Mrs. Johnson goes to bed, I sneak back into the kitchen and turn the computer on. The green glow illuminates the entire room, and I open my mail program.

I start a new message and hold my fingers over the keyboard. Force down a finger onto the letter *D* and then *e* until I have typed "Dear Dad" for the first time since the explosion.

So many words come into my head and then disappear like mist. It's too soon to talk about Meriwether and her mom. Too hard to describe what happened with the Angustus Church protesters. Too embarrassing to tell him how I handled my anger over the posters.

Everything I write seems false or stupid.

But I close my eyes anyway and let my fingers find the proper keys.

Dear Dad:

Remember Sam's church? Church of the Nativity? The one by the bay that has a shell sculpture in front of it? And a fountain in the garden? I went there with

Sam, and we lit candles and said prayers for every-one. For you, Dad. For every soldier. For every orphan. It didn't matter we aren't Catholics.

We sang one song I know you like. "Peace Is Flow-ing Like a River." Can't you hear it now, how the words float over you and the weight of them is nothing? You can breathe. Breathe with your eyes closed, floating on water? Peace like that?

Dad, that's what I feel when I think how you are coming home.

Love,

Jess

There are other things to say. But for right now, this is all I can say. Afraid the words won't sound right, I don't reread them. I press send before I change my mind.

NINETEEN

AT BREAKFAST Mrs. Johnson blows air over her coffee to cool it. In front of her on the kitchen table is a newspaper. Unfolded.

From the doorway, I can read the banner. *Clementine Times.*

I slump into a chair. "Is it bad?"

"Define bad." Mrs. Johnson stirs a heap of sugar into her coffee. She pushes the paper my way. Above the fold, a photo looks familiar. It's the one of the orphanage that I sent to the reporter. The goat's been cropped out, though. That's not good. The goat meant something. Maybe the reporter didn't understand the rest of the story either.

The caption reads "Local Teens Form Charitable Organization: Good Intentions, Uneasy Outcome in Kabul. See Story in People and Places, page 3."

I turn the page as if I'm going to uncover an IED underneath that will explode when I touch the paper.

"Jess," Mrs. Johnson says, "don't take this to heart. Hear? You don't let them get you down. And you don't give up on your dad, either." Mrs. Johnson wipes up all of Cara's leftover crumbs with a damp cloth.

Mrs. Johnson, encouraging me? Things must be bad. Really bad.

I begin reading on page three. "After Fort Spencer soldiers were deployed, three local teens — all children of military personnel — joined forces to create an organization to help orphans in Afghanistan." The article goes on to explain how we started. Then I read the next part. "But as is often the case, charitable intentions can go awry. On July 5 the orphanage was attacked by a car bomb, the timing of which also resulted in destruction of a U.S. Army Humvee and led to the deaths of two soldiers from Fort Spencer, Corporal Miranda Scott and Private Josh Davis. (See story on Corporal Scott's Funeral Disrupted by the Angustus Church on page 1.) It also injured Master Sergeant Westmark of Clementine. Some press reports have suggested complicity by U.S. troops in the attack, and though an investigation is ongoing, the consensus to date is that the U.S. troops fired no shots and are not culpable. The fate of the poster child for Operation Oleander's publicity campaign is unknown as of this writing. The orphanage — or what is left of it — is officially off-limits to members of the military.

"Critics of grass-roots efforts like Operation Oleander, particularly those that have a military face to them, say they are risking the safety of aid workers and undermining the very causes they purportedly are trying to help."

My eyes blur. The article goes on to quote some charitable leaders who fear "any connection with U.S. soldiers, no matter how benign, not only creates unnecessary risk to the soldiers but leads to significantly increased chances that their intended aid recipients will be targeted by insurgents. The July 5 attack on the orphanage appears to be an example of such targeting. In the aftermath of the attack, Operation Oleander is regrouping and determining how best to assist charitable efforts in Afghanistan. For now, Operation Oleander founder Jess Westmark advises that the larger, more established international relief organizations are probably the most advised vehicles for assisting humanitarian efforts in Afghanistan. In the meantime, People and Places salutes Jess Westmark and Sam Butler, Commander Butler's son, for their efforts." Misguided efforts, that's what Ms. Sanchez-Ryan emphasizes. And she has to point out that Sam is the commander's son.

"There's more." Mrs. Johnson points to the front page

again. Below the fold, a photo of angry protesters glares off the page. There I am, shot from behind, tearing the edge of the poster like I'm playing a game of capture the flag.

"Can you tell it's me?" I ask.

"No, and thank heavens no one ratted you out, either."

The caption under the photo reads "Unknown counterprotester seeks to disrupt peaceful, though contentious, antiwar protest at the funeral of one of our own, Corporal Scott of Fort Spencer." The article headline, in tall, black letters: "Angustus Church Protests Local Funeral."

Counterprotester? I take a deep breath.

I refold the newspaper and press the creases, making it look unopened, unread. So much for the article highlighting the positive efforts of our operation. Now even the name Operation Oleander has a bad sound to it, like the sound of a secret military society in a dictatorship. It was just as well Commander Butler shut our fundraising down for now. After the article, no one would want to be associated with it. Or me.

Shouldn't Sam be calling me? Or Commander Butler? To yell at me? But they don't. It's too much to hope they didn't see the article.

It'll be all over town, and Fort Spencer.

"I'm going for a walk."

Mrs. Johnson nods. This time, she doesn't even ask me where I'm going.

I pull on one of Dad's old ball caps to cover my face and head out of the house.

At the JifMart, I buy an extra-large frozen slush drink, the kind that makes my teeth freeze. I sit outside on the curb and drink it, watching cars come and go. Wondering what to do now.

A shadow falls over me, and I squint up, afraid someone has recognized me.

It's the blond girl from the PX, from the funeral. Sam told me her name.

Aria.

"I saw the article in the newspaper," she says. Her toenails are painted parrot bright, and she's carrying a bag on one hip. A carton of milk pokes out the top.

Just my luck.

"Oh, that. It wasn't very good." It was horrible. "We still don't know if Warda's alive. The girl on the poster." The PX fundraising seems so long ago, and it's only been days.

"I remember her."

Sure, she remembers how I flung everything off the table and wouldn't let her assist.

"I was thinking about what I could do to help," she says.

My face goes warm. "I'm sorry I —"

Aria touches my arm. "It wasn't anything."

"The commander ordered us to stand down for now. I don't know when — if — we'll start again. Maybe it wasn't doing anything. Not the right way."

"Don't say that. It's good."

Aria sits next to me on the curb and cradles the groceries in her arms.

"How do you know?" I've asked myself that question. "We helped a couple of orphans. Then look what happened." Everything gone in a puff of smoke.

Aria twists a braided band around her thin wrist. "If you don't help, you won't know what could happen. You aren't responsible for everything. Just what you do. It's the starfish method."

Starfish? What does she mean?

"You've never heard of it?" she asks.

"No."

"It's about a man who sees a little boy down on the beach before sunrise. He's watching the boy tossing starfish that had been trapped by the tide back into the sea. The man sees starfish stretching for miles down the beach. He asks the little boy why he's doing that when it's clear he can't save most of them. And the little boy says, 'I can save this one.' He tosses another one into the sea. And another. It's like that."

I nod and shield my eyes from the bright sunlight. I bet the critics from Ms. Sanchez-Ryan's article would find something wrong with the starfish story, too. Like maybe if you couldn't save them all, how can you morally save only one? And how do you decide which one to save? Besides, maybe it's your fault all those starfish needed to be rescued in the first place.

"So, may I help?"

"Why do you want to?" I ask. After everything — the explosion, the investigation, the newspaper article, and the protests. Why now?

"Because I want to do something. My dad's out there too."

I nod. In the distance, cars speed down the oleander-lined road. The people in them are moving on, buying milk and going to Disney World. Making plans.

"You really want to?"

Aria nods.

"Okay. No promises."

We walk together to Madrid Street, where I turn off for home. Aria's starfish story keeps running in my head. When I get home, I get on the computer and look up charities that work in Afghanistan.

Mr. Johnson calls before supper. Mrs. Johnson stands in the kitchen stirring spaghetti sauce while she talks to him. Cara's drawing on her paper at the table. Sitting across from her, I plug in my earbuds and tune them all out. I'm trying to write a letter to Meriwether on the computer. But the words aren't coming.

Mrs. Johnson taps me on the shoulder. She motions for me to take out my earbuds.

"What?"

"Frank wants to talk to you," she says.

I frown. "Mr. Johnson?"

"Yes, come on, take the phone." She stretches out the cord to hand me the phone with one hand while she holds a spoon in the sauce with the other.

Puzzled, I pick up and say hello.

"Hi, Jess." I almost expect him to ask how much I've grown since they deployed, but he doesn't. He's Dad's friend, and the kind of soldier who doesn't spend a lot of time chatting with dependents, especially children. His usual greeting on coming over to watch a game with Dad or to chuck a few hot dogs or brats on the grill is "Hi" and "How much taller are you?" Sometimes he'll say, "Mostly I let Libby do the talking." And if she's in earshot, she rolls her eyes.

"I talked to your mom yesterday," he says. "I was

OPERATION OLEANDER ★ 169

hoping to talk to your dad. Your mom put the receiver up to his ear, and I talked *at* him for a few minutes. First time I've ever been able to do that without him cutting me off. I don't know if he understood or heard me, but I thought it would be good, you know, for him to hear voices from his unit out here. Those of us who were with him."

Those not dead.

"There's something I want to send you," Frank said.

"I—I don't want anything from Afghanistan," I say. Just word on Warda. Mr. Johnson's so quiet on the other end of the line that I think we've been cut off.

"I think you might change your mind," he finally says. "When you see. On the day of the explosion—"

"I don't want to talk about it."

Around me, the room gets very white, like being inside an explosion.

Mrs. Johnson hovers at the edge of my vision, folding and unfolding a dishcloth.

"You need to," he says. "Your dad was proud of us—he was proud of you. *Is* proud. He had us all doing our duty over here. The orphanage was separate, extra. But you could tell it was—it *is*—special to him. To all of us."

The way he says it, it sounds as if there's more bad news. "Is Warda okay?" Maybe this is why he called. To tell me she died too.

"I'm trying to get word," Mr. Johnson says. "Nothing yet. We'll let you know. Why don't you put the missus back on the phone?"

"Here, Mrs. Johnson." I hold up the phone.

Mr. Johnson's call gives me a sliver of hope, and yet, when I hand the phone over to Mrs. Johnson, it's as if I'm left without having talked to him at all.

The computer screen flashes at me. Like a warning message. The letter to Meriwether refuses to be written. Not even when I could tell her that Caden asked about her.

I ride my bicycle past Meriwether's house. The drapes are still drawn. No car sits in the driveway. Nothing out front. The house sits vacant like something abandoned. How funny that houses seem to know they're empty.

Maybe they're visiting relatives. Maybe they spent a night out of town. Maybe Mr. Scott took Meriwether to Disney. Or Universal Studios. Something to cheer them both, even a little.

Along the bike path that lines the main road, a row of oleander separates us from the cars. I head for the beach. There, I park my bike and walk along the edge of the shore.

Meriwether was right in a way. Naming a charity after a poisonous plant was a little odd, maybe. Yet it still makes sense to me in a way another name wouldn't.

Oleander roots and grows from Afghanistan to Apalachicola — beautiful, delicate, but also with a dark side, one not to be trusted. Just like people. Or some beliefs. Yet it also thrives in the harshest heat when more tender plants wilt and timid colors fade in the harsh sun.

If Warda survives, oleander is the appropriate symbol for the operation. But could I make it take root again in damaged soil? After the explosion and death and injury there and here, how is Operation Oleander supposed to respond?

How am I? Is it really as simple as Aria says?

One starfish?

Is Warda that one starfish?

TWENTY

ON MONDAY a brown-wrapped package arrives.
As if it brings bad news, Mrs. Johnson drops it on
the kitchen table, where I'm helping Cara mold putty ani-
mals.

"This is for you," she says.

The return address says Afghanistan. I can tell without touching the box. "It's from Mr. Johnson."

Mrs. Johnson sniffs. "But it's addressed to you. He
said he was mailing something to you." With that, she
pivots on her espadrille heel, not an easy move, and un-
loads a meal's worth of plastic containers and foil-covered
packages from a paper bag. Takeout again.

The package feels lightweight, but the contents shuf-
fle from one end to the other when I shake it. I rip the
end where the package had been stapled and then taped

over to keep the ends of the metal staples from catching. Inside, clusters of photographs are banded together, a wrinkled note on top.

I unfold the note. It reads,

> See? These are the things that Operation Oleander did for the orphanage. A lot was destroyed in the bombing. But they can rebuild. They are rebuilding.

I stop reading Mr. Johnson's note and thumb through the stack of photos.

> Here are some of the children. One of the girls, the one on the left, was killed.

I stare at the girl for a long time before moving on.

> Under the photos, there are some cards for you and the others.

On the back, someone printed our names in English and penned a short note of thanks. Rough, childlike scrawls — signatures? — appear underneath.

> And, Jess, I did get some news from the orphanage director. I didn't want to go back there myself – you understand. Couldn't. After what happened, that area's off-limits for soldiers.

But the director sent something from Warda in
the little blue pouch. It's for you. You'll be able to
tell what it is. Warda knows about your dad, too.
I told the orphanage director that he's alive and
to make sure she knows that.

I sit back, close my eyes.

Warda's alive. If only I'd been able to tell Ms.
Sanchez-Ryan. Maybe the article could have ended on
a positive note. Maybe it would have made a difference
in how she wrote the article.

I read on.

Warda had run down into the cellar looking for
some vegetable peelings for the goat. That crazy
goat – can you believe it?

Operation Oleander's goat saved Warda. Even though
the operation drew the enemy to the orphanage.

I recognize Warda right away, by her eyes.

A small blue cloth bag slides onto the table from the
box. I unknot the strings and pull open the gathers, careful not to break the cords. A creamy, smooth stone nestles
inside. The way the stone was formed, a seam runs along
the edge as if it had folded over onto itself and hardened
that way. A flower captured forever in the moment just
before blooming — that's what it looks like.

Not just any bud, either. An oleander bud. Does Warda understand Operation Oleander? Does she know why I picked the oleander as the symbol for our efforts? Is that why she sent along the stone shaped like a bud?

I close my fingers over the stone, pretend the bud is a seed. A seed in the dark soil of my fist.

The last package of photos is wrapped in a note and held by a rubber band. Bold, uneven words lope across the unlined page, as if Mr. Johnson's sentences were running uphill and trying to catch their breath as he wrote.

> These photos are the ones from Mrs. Scott's camera, the last ones she took. They survived the explosion. The camera was blown clear acros the courtyard.

Mrs. Scott's photos. What she saw in the last minutes of her life through the viewfinder of her camera.

His letter goes on:

> I was going to mail them to Mr. Scott along with the rest of Mrs. Scott's belongings. Word came he didn't want us to return the camera. So we've given it to the orphanage. But we weren't sure what to do with the photos and the memory card. We didn't want to destroy them. We thought of

your dad, but he's in Germany and soon to be stateside. That leaves you, Miss Jess, because there is no one else who would appreciate more what these photos mean. So we turn them over to the custody of Operation Oleander.

Sincerely,

Frank Johnson

With shaking fingers, I slip off the rubber band. The first photo shows several of the girls playing with a ball. Another one was taken outside the orphanage doors, in the courtyard. That's where the bomb exploded a few minutes or so later. Had the army looked at these photos as part of the investigation into what happened? Or were these duplicates and, somewhere, Mrs. Scott's photos had become part of the official record?

The last photo is of Warda by herself. She's standing alone near the doorway, her hand on the wall. Oleander bushes grow on one side. Warda stares right into the photo, as if Mrs. Scott — Corporal Scott — had gotten her to look into her eyes and the camera lens wasn't even separating them. That's how intense the look is. How close.

I clutch the photo to my chest.

Almost as if they'd both known. *Impossible.*

Mr. Johnson was partly wrong, though. There is someone else who will appreciate these photos as much as me. Maybe more.

Meriwether.

"Mrs. Johnson, we have to get copies of these photos made. Today."

"Hold on. What are you talking about?"

"Mr. Johnson sent photos and letters from the orphanage."

Mrs. Johnson shakes her head. "That Frank, he's a sentimental one. Never know it to look at him."

"You don't understand. The best news. Warda's still alive." I hold up the photograph of Warda that Mr. Johnson had sent, one of the ones taken by Mrs. Scott.

Mrs. Johnson squints at the photo. "That's the girl in the photos at the fundraiser?"

"Yes, she was there the first day my dad and the others took supplies."

The stone I keep hidden away. That's my secret.

"Mrs. Scott took this photo," I say. "All of these."

Mrs. Johnson touches the photos, as if touching them makes them more real. "I'll be . . ."

"We have to get copies made. Now."

Mrs. Johnson frowns at me. "It can wait until after lunch."

"Now. I want to go now. I want to get them to Meriwether."

TWENTY-ONE

AFTER WE get back with the duplicate photos, I phone Sam first, afraid Commander Butler will answer the phone and say something about the article in the *Clementine Times*.

But Sam answers.

"You won't believe what I have."

"What?" he asks.

"Photos. Photos of the orphanage that Meriwether's mother took that day." The day of the explosion.

"Really?"

"Yes, Mr. Johnson sent them. I've made copies. A set for you. A set for Meriwether. Will you come with me?"

"Where?"

"To Meriwether's house. I want you to be there when

I give them to her." All of us together. All of Operation Oleander.

Sam doesn't answer right away. He shuffles from one foot to the other. I can tell even through the phone line.

"Okay, I'm coming,"

Sam meets me at the corner of Madrid, and we bike to Meriwether's house together. Like we used to.

This time the Scotts' car is there, parked on the street. The curtains are open. But in the driveway there's a moving van. It's backed up to the carport, and men are loading it with boxes and furniture wrapped in heavy quilting.

The thud of the moving boxes echoes in my heart. I am the day lilies Meriwether dug up. The missing dragonfly garden stake. I am all the things being ripped away.

They have to move off post. Everyone knows that. But not so soon. They're going farther, to South Carolina, for now.

"Did you know they were moving today?" I ask Sam.

He nods. "Mom told me."

"Why didn't you say anything?" We are best friends, Meriwether and me. And Sam.

He shakes his head. "Couldn't."

"More duty, honor, country?" Is he just like his dad after all?

"No," he says. "It was one more sad thing."

I blink back tears. No crying here.

"Come on," I say.

We pick our way through the chairs and tables waiting to be loaded. Dodge packers and movers who work like robots, knowing how to be efficient.

Inside the living room, it already feels like a stranger's house.

"Jess, Sam." It's Mr. Scott. He waves us toward the hallway and the kitchen beyond, where the lighting shows off the azure tiles.

My heart beats hard. The last time I saw Meriwether was at the funeral. The last time I was here before that, I tried to give Meriwether an album. An album of photos of us. It's back at home in a drawer. If I'd known they were moving today, I'd have brought it. Even if Meriwether rejected it. I could have hidden it in the moving van, and she'd find it later, when she might want it.

Sam and I join Mr. Scott, who's standing next to the sink, a cup in his hand. He looks like he's having a morning cup like any other morning and the chaos around him doesn't bother him. As if he doesn't see any of it.

"We have something for Meriwether. And for you." I hold out the packet of processed photographs.

"Meriwether?" Mr. Scott calls out the back window.

When Meriwether walks in, we all stand straight and silent in four corners of the kitchen, walled in by the blue tiles that always made me smile.

"Mr. Johnson sent me these photos —"

"I don't want them." Meriwether folds her arms.

"They're —"

"I told you I don't want them." She and her dad don't look at the package.

"I can explain." I look to Sam, and he nods but doesn't say anything. "That day, that day at the orphanage, your mom took photos."

Meriwether's foot is tapping, and her arms are so tight across her chest, her hands are clenched. My hands are shaking, just a little, but enough so the paper bag crinkles. "She took photos of the children and my dad. They are the last images she captured on film." They are what she saw.

Mr. Scott clears his throat.

"Photos of the orphanage? Really, Jess?" Meriwether's eyes whip like frothy wind-tossed waves. "What makes you think I want them?"

"Because your mom took them."

Mr. Scott's hands clench together in front of him. Meriwether doesn't budge.

"I'll just leave them here, on the counter." Where the movers won't throw them out as trash. "We'll go, Sam and me. Please write and tell me where you are." South Carolina.

I ease the photos onto the counter space, and Sam and I leave through the front hallway.

Finally, outside, I can breathe again.

"It's not your fault, Jess," Sam says after we start biking back toward my house.

I nod, but I don't believe him. Not really.

"I'm going to talk to your dad again," I say.

He hits the brakes and stops. "What?"

"I'm going to ask him about restarting Operation Oleander."

Sam gives me one of his looks, the looks I have trouble reading. "Okay."

Okay? That's it? He doesn't argue. I don't believe him.

"I've been thinking about what else we could do. For when your dad lifts the ban. I did some research online. We could donate everything we get to a national organization that provides for an Afghanistan aid center," I say.

"I'm listening." Sam twists the handlebars on his bike.

"That way there's no link between the U.S. military and the orphans. I liked knowing that what we had done we did ourselves. But it's more important that the supplies get where they're needed. The safest way for everyone."

"It might work."

★ ★ ★

The next morning, I head over to the PX. The table for the snack sales is already unfolded and in its place. I just need to unlock the closet and unpack, then add some information about the Afghanistan Aid organization I researched.

"Reporting for duty," a voice says.

I look up.

Sam's standing in front of me, saluting.

Next to him, Aria clutches a stiff poster board. On it she's made a collage with photos of Warda and the others.

Suddenly, I am standing on the edge of a cliff again. Dizzy, the way I felt when Meriwether told me about deleting her mother's voice-mail message. When I think about the destruction done by the insurgents, the bombings, the anger and hatred of the Angustus protesters with their signs. Both sides of hatred, each claiming the other is evil.

"Aria, do you agree to the membership duties of Operation Oleander."

"Yes," she says.

"Duties?" Sam asks.

"Like duty, honor, country. Only ours are different in some ways. Giving isn't always only a good thing — I know that now. Even good motives lead to unintended consequences. But I'm not giving up. And neither is Operation Oleander."

I continue. "Giving matters. Each small gift together.

Maybe that's all that matters." Giving without the thought of return. Not for a gold star. Or to make Dad proud. Not even for the internal joy. I distrust my own heart.

"Father Killen said that we should do it, follow the form. And the substance will come," I say.

"He was talking about prayer, Jess," Sam said. "He always says that."

"I know that. But giving is a form of prayer too."

Through the fabric of my pocket, I feel the stone. A stone that is my own gift, my own shared prayer of life.

"If one orphan benefits, isn't that good enough?" Aria asks.

I salute them back.

Yes.

That afternoon, it's raining again. I've taken an umbrella and walked to the street in my flip-flops to get the mail.

Mr. Scott pulls his car up to the curb, and Meriwether bolts from the passenger side without an umbrella. I stand on the sidewalk, not sure whether to go to her or back away. I wait for her anger to crest over me like a rogue wave, my body stiff.

"Don't. You're getting soaked," I say.

But Meriwether grabs onto me in a hug that crushes my lungs.

"Jess" is all she says. I hug her back. Without her

telling me, I know the photos her mom took are going with her. They are the gift she can hold on to.

"Wait, don't leave," I tell her. I give her my umbrella and run for the house.

Mrs. Johnson says, "What the — ?" when I crash into the living room and down the hall, my flip-flops squeaking from the rain. In my room I find the album still in the tote bag. I race back outside.

"Here. Take this. It's for you. It's an album. Of us. I've been saving photos since last year."

Meriwether shelters the album as she carries it to the car and stashes it inside, out of the rain.

Then she reaches for something in the back seat.

"I want you to have some of these."

Day lilies.

"Please take care of them," Meriwether says. "Mom loved them."

A flash of lightning singes the air.

The thunder booms, and Meriwether and I hug hard one last time before she leaves.

From under the dry carport, I turn and wave at the Scotts. The rain is coming down so hard, I can't see them through their car windshield. But I know they are waving too.

I hold the burlap-wrapped day lilies tight in my

arms. They're my orphans too, like Warda and the other children.

The Scotts' car turns at the end of the block. Later, whoever moves into their house won't know the day lilies left in the yard belonged to Mrs. Scott. They won't know that she planted them carefully, babied them. Or how much she loved them. Whoever moves in next might even replace them with other landscaping.

But I know what they're called. *Hemerocallis.* From the Greek for "beauty for a day" because each bloom lasts for only about twenty-four hours. Just a single day, and I think about what Mrs. Scott said: "Life is too short not to plant flowers."

I won't forget these links between us. Between Mrs. Scott and Meriwether. Between Meriwether and me. Between us and the orphans in Afghanistan whom we will never know in person.

I will call them all by name.